FOWL MURDER

A KENYA KANGA MYSTERY

VICTORIA TAIT

KANGA
PRESS

Dedication
For Cassandra, Allie & Dad
for helping bring this book together

For more information visit VictoriaTait.com

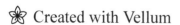 Created with Vellum

STYLE & KISWAHILI GLOSSARY

The main character, Mama Rose, has a British upbringing and she uses British phrases.

Kiswahili words are used to add to the richness and authenticity of the setting and characters, and most are linked to this Glossary.

- *Asante* Thank you
- *Bob* Slang for Kenyan shilling, currency of Kenya
- *Boda-Boda* Motorbike used as a taxi
- *Boran* Breed of cattle with a distinctive hump at the base of the neck

- *Bwana* Sir, a term of respect used for an older man
- *Chai* Tea consisting of bags or leaves boiled in a mixture of $2/3^{rd}$ water and $1/3^{rd}$ milk
- *Chamgei* Hello in the Kalenjin tribal language
- *Dawa* Medicine
- *Dhobi Room* Laundry, or back room for domestic chores.
- *Habari* Greeting used like hello but meaning 'What news?'
- *Hapana* No
- *Kanga* Colourful cotton fabric (also Swahili for guinea fowl)
- *Kikoi* Brightly coloured cotton material, garment or sarong
- *Mabati* Corrugated iron sheeting, often used for roofing
- *Mitumba* Second-hand clothes, shoes and fabric market. Literal meaning is 'bundles' derived from the plastic wrapped packages the donated clothing arrives in
- *Mpesa* Mobile money sent from one phone account to another

- *Mzee* Elder
- *Mzungu* European/White person
- *Pesa* Money
- *Pole* Sorry
- *Pole Pole* Slowly (slowly)
- *Sawa (sawa)* Fine, all good, no worries.
- *Shamba* Farm, garden or area of cultivated land
- *Shuka* Thin, brightly coloured blanket in bright checked colours, where red is often the dominant colour. Also used as a sarong or throw
- *Sufuria* A flat based, deep-sided cooking pot, usually metal with no handles
- *Syce* A groom/someone who looks after horses
- *Tusker & Whitecap* Brands of beer brewed by East African Breweries
- *Ugali M*aize flour dish, cooked until it reaches a stiff, dough-like consistency
- *Uhuru* A flower farm on the slopes of Mount Kenya

CHAPTER ONE

Through our eyes we observe the fabric, the skin, the cover of the world, and we do not question the reality presented to us. So look! Scrutinise what lies beneath the surface, for there the truth exists.

The bullet merely grazed Rose's arm, but it tore through her peaceful existence. On the surface, Rose was a respectable European woman in her early sixties, with frizzy white hair, grooved skin and a lanky frame.

She lived contentedly with her husband Craig in Nanyuki, a small town two hundred kilometres north of Nairobi, the capital of Kenya. But the ghosts of her past still haunted her.

Only occasionally did she remember the young man whose life she had taken, but the guilt of her action drove her to support and protect people and animals alike in her local community.

It was March and there had been no rain for three months. The scrubland around Nanyuki was shrivelled, and the ground baked hard. Wispy grass had long since been consumed by roving herds of ragged sheep and goats, and only cactus plants, twiggy bushes and thorny acacia trees survived.

Rose was collecting leaves from a milkweed bush, which she would dry and give to local people who could not afford expensive medicines, to relieve their headaches.

She half stood. Thwack. She froze, her senses alive. Was that a gun? Something punched her left arm. Something she could neither see nor hear, but her upper arm burned. If it was a shot, would there be more? Should she try to run? No point. She couldn't outrun a bullet.

"Oh, my goodness! Are you all right?" shouted a female voice. It was familiar, calling to her from her past.

She turned cautiously, clutching her arm, and was confronted by an oval face, topped with a yellow and brown kanga turban, peering wide-eyed over a thorny hedge.

"Rose! My friend. Heavens, did I hit you? I heard your cry."

Rose could not remember uttering a sound, and now her voice dried up.

"Thabiti," shouted the woman beyond the hedge. "Quick, help Rose, I think I've shot her."

Guinea Fowl Cottage was a small, single storey colonial-style property with a dusty yard at the rear and a vibrant garden at the front. Rose was escorted onto the veranda, a raised wooden platform which extended across the front of the house.

It was a versatile space with a cedar dining table and a wicker sofa and chairs. The latter had plump white cushions decorated with guinea fowl feather motifs. A corrugated metal roof provided shade and relief from the oppressive March sun.

Rose clutched the dressing on her arm and winced in pain. She felt her scalp prickle as she surveyed her friend and asked, in a hoarse voice, "Aisha, old friend. What on earth are you doing here?"

The two women had met as children on their first day at a prestigious Nairobi girl's school. Rose had been an untamed country girl, and Aisha was the school's first African pupil.

Aisha had been studious and worked her way to become a top human and civil rights lawyer. She'd also developed into a flamboyant character who now displayed her full figure in a bright kanga dress, with her matching signature turban head wrap. She smiled widely, but Rose noticed her twisting a large gold ring.

"Do you like the house? We needed a break from Nairobi, which is so dull in winter. And I thought Nanyuki's fresh highland air would be good for us." Aisha's smile drooped at the edges.

"But it's not winter yet," responded Rose, suspecting Aisha was avoiding the real reason for her return. "You sneak into Nanyuki without telling your old friends and take this tiny cottage. It's not your style."

Flustered, Aisha shrilled, "Ah, here comes Thabiti with my drink."

Aisha's son, Thabiti, looked to be in his late teens or early twenties and had an oval face which matched his mother's. He wore his hair short and neat, and a trim moustache and beard encircled his mouth. He handed his mother a glass of brandy.

"Where's Rose's drink?" Aisha's voice was sharp.

Thabiti looked down at the floor. "Doris is bringing it."

A bird-like maid with a pointed nose, quick darting eyes, and two knots of hair protruding from the sides of her head, like additional ears, rushed onto the veranda. She placed a china teacup and saucer beside Rose and backed away.

Rose turned to Thabiti and said kindly, "I was asking your mother why you'd moved back to Nanyuki."

"I suppose she blamed…"

"Now, now," interrupted Aisha. "There's no need to bore Rose with all that." She rubbed the back of her neck. "My dear Rose, I told you, we just needed to get out of Nairobi. I really am sorry for shooting you, but I swear, I didn't see anyone when I looked over the hedge."

Rose leaned forward and patted Aisha's arm. "Don't worry, no real harm's been done." She winced again as her arm throbbed. "I guess I must have been squatting down out of sight. But why a gun? And what were you doing shooting into the bush?"

Aisha shuffled her ample bottom in her wicker chair. "I was practising shooting some empty cans Thabiti had placed on the fence, in front of the hedge. But I'm afraid I'm not a great shot. You know I've always been better with my head than my hands."

Aisha lifted her hands, but quickly returned them to her lap. In a serious tone, she said, "But I could have killed you. I don't like guns. I never have. Not since… the incident." She shivered.

Rose also felt a chill run through her, and she wrapped her hands round her teacup. She forced herself to ask, "So why do you have one?"

"It was issued to me, because of my work with the EACC, the Ethics and Anti-Corruption Commission."

Rose raised her eyebrows. "But surely that's not standard procedure?"

"No, it's not…" Thabiti replied.

But Aisha interrupted her son again. "Thabiti." She took a deep breath. "Go inside and let me catch up with Mama Rose."

Thabiti looked at his mother and then down at the wooden floor.

He turned and trudged towards the house with his hands in his pockets. In the doorway, he looked back at his mother with a wrinkled brow before shaking his head and leaving them alone.

Rose turned to Aisha, who gazed out towards the garden. "I'm no fool. I know something is wrong. And drawing a veil over your problem only hides it. Things may have been different between us since… the incident, but I'm still your friend. And I might be able to help you."

CHAPTER TWO

Rose was sitting with her childhood friend, Aisha Onyango, on the veranda of Guinea Fowl Cottage, which Aisha had rented in the market town of Nanyuki, in Kenya.

Aisha swirled brandy around her glass and reminisced, "I remember how we met. Two outcasts brought together at the birth of a new Kenya. I know for your family, and other European settlers, it was a time of uncertainty as you lost friends, lands and a way of life. But for my family it was so exciting: a new Kenya, with security, harmony and economic prosperity for all. The glorious vision of Independence."

Aisha's eyes sparkled as she looked at Rose. "And I was the first African pupil at the Kenya High School for Girls. My father was so proud, God rest his soul."

Rose could discern the face of the young girl etched beneath the woman in front of her, as Aisha continued, "I still remember the words of his colleague, Josiah Kariuki. 'Every Kenyan man, woman and child is entitled to a decent and just living. That is a birthright. It is not a privilege. He is entitled as far as is humanly possible to equal educational, job and health opportunities irrespective of his parentage, race, creed, or his area of origin in this land. If that is so, deliberate efforts should be made to eliminate all obstacles that today stand in the way of this just goal. That is the primary task of the machinery called government: our government'," quoted Aisha.

"No wonder he was assassinated," commented Rose dryly.

"My father believed this. So do I. I love Kenya." Aisha lifted her arms into the air as if celebrating Independence all over again.

Rose scoffed. "You love a dream. In reality, people in prominent positions fancy that what belongs to the country can be taken for their own personal gain. Did you see the wheelbarrow article in *The Star* last week?"

Aisha dropped her arms. "It was one of my investigations. The Bungoma County Agricultural Ministry bought several wheelbarrows and claimed they paid a hundred thousand Kenyan shillings for each, when the going rate is five thousand shillings."

"Exactly. And where did the other ninety-five thousand shillings go? I bet it was into the pockets of local officials. So will they be held to account?" Rose raised her eyebrows.

"I can't say. The results of my investigation are with the court, and it has to decide if further action should be taken." Aisha's face was pinched and full of tension.

"That'll be a no then." Rose felt as frustrated as her friend appeared to be. Whilst she had enough to eat and drink, many of those she helped in Nanyuki prison or at the teenage mother's charity did not.

She returned to the topic of Aisha's return. "Does your work with the EACC have anything to do with your move to Nanyuki?"

"I am working on a new project," Aisha mumbled.

Rose leaned forward. "And is it the reason you left Nairobi?"

Aisha sat back and said, "Not exactly. I don't blame Thabiti, although he believes I do, but he is in serious trouble at university. They've accused him of assaulting a girl, but he swears it wasn't him. A witness saw a man with the same build as Thabiti running away from the scene. And he was wearing a distinctive red and white beanie hat. Thabiti has one, but now he can't find it."

"Oh dear, so what's going to happen?" Rose sipped her tea.

"The university is investigating the claims, but other students started harassing him, having already judged him to be guilty. I was worried. You see, he gets very anxious and isn't strong enough to deal with a situation like this. I wasn't happy about him returning, but that's irrelevant as the university asked him to stay away until the matter's resolved. I hoped moving to Nanyuki would benefit us all. We were happy here for a while, when Thabiti and Pearl were children."

Rose hoped Thabiti was innocent of the charges, but she still suspected this was not the real reason for Aisha's sudden reappearance in Nanyuki. It was more likely to be something related to Aisha's work. Aisha had joined the EACC on its inception in 2003, leaving Nanyuki and returning to Nairobi. Clearly, she still felt strongly about her role, and the country Kenya had the potential to become.

Aisha broke into Rose's thoughts. "I'm currently working with the Kenya Anti-Poaching Unit, who are investigating the hunting of elephants and the illegal ivory trade. It's an issue high on the government's agenda since President Kenyatta is setting fire to over a hundred tons of confiscated ivory next month, at the culmination of the Giants Club summit. The conference is looking at ways to protect Africa's elephant population and at least four African heads of state planning to attend. Did you know it's being held at the Mount Kenya Hotel and Spa, just outside Nanyuki?"

Rose nodded and lifted her cup of tea.

Aisha leaned forward, taking hold of Rose's free hand, but she was unable to look her in the eye as she said, "My initial work included looking back at the 1970s, at the period just after the hunting ban. And I've been reading through my father's papers from that time, which included the incident you and I were involved in at Ol Kilima Ranch."

Rose grabbed her hand away from Aisha's and, as she did, she dropped her cup. It shattered, shooting shards of coloured china across the wooden floor. She sat transfixed and rigid in her seat.

Aisha ignored the smashed crockery and said, in a sympathetic tone, "I'm sorry. I realise this isn't easy for you. It was such a frightening time."

A figure dashed from the house with a brush made of dried reeds and swiftly swept up the scattered pieces.

Aisha sat up. "Doris, more tea for Rose, please."

Rose felt the presence of a ghost from her past. She spoke quietly and deliberately. "But that happened forty years ago. Why does it matter now?"

Aisha lifted a scuffed grey box file from beside her chair. She tapped it and said, "These are papers from the days following the incident, and they indicate a relationship beginning to develop between certain government officials and organised criminal groups. Up until now, events such as the one at Ol Kilima have been glossed over. They need to be fully investigated."

Rose felt dizzy. Did Aisha really mean to drag up her past? Aisha had defended her, protected her from those who wanted her to pay for her crime. So why would she want to re-open the case now?

CHAPTER THREE

R ose needed to escape from Guinea Fowl Cottage, but she didn't trust her legs to carry her. She nodded gratefully at the housemaid, Doris, who brought her a fresh cup of steaming tea.

It was half-past five and the intensity of the day's heat was waning. From nearby she heard the cries of a baby, mixed with the char-grilled smell of maize being roasted on an open charcoal fire. She felt the remnants of sweat tingle her skin as she forced herself to focus on the everyday sounds of life around her.

The arrival of a pretty, willowy African girl on the arm of an attractive and well-groomed man with an ostentatious air saved her from further discussions with Aisha.

"Evening, Mrs Onyango," remarked the man, who Rose considered to be in his early thirties. He certainly looked a good five years older than the girl he propelled forward, with his arm on the small of her back. Rose presumed she was Pearl, Aisha's daughter.

Aisha replied, "Hello Francis. This is an old friend of mine, Rose Hardie."

"Pleased to meet you," he said, with only the briefest glance in Rose's direction, before he addressed Aisha again. "We're attending an official dinner in Nyeri tonight."

"I still expect Pearl back by midnight," declared Aisha.

"I'm not Cinderella," Pearl muttered.

"What was that?" quipped Aisha. "You're still my responsibility and I want you safely home and tucked up in bed. Francis, please be careful driving back. The road between Nyeri and

Kiganjo is treacherous with all those hills and bends."

Pearl looked down at her shoes and twirled a brown and gold hair braid, with a pretty silver clip and guinea fowl feather, between her fingers and thumb.

"You might well look at your shoes, my girl. So inappropriate with that high heel and open toe."

Pearl jerked upright. "But Ma…"

Francis's ears turned pink, and he growled, "I bought those for Pearl, and they're very striking and expensive."

Aisha scowled. "Very well. Have a good evening but remember to be back by midnight."

Pearl sighed as Francis propelled her through the veranda door.

"The last time I saw Pearl, she was just a girl," remarked Rose. "You must be proud of her. She's an attractive young woman."

"But what does she want? What does she do? At her age I had already qualified as a lawyer and was acting for clients in court. She reads magazines, sketches, goes to the salon and chats with friends. She has no drive, no ambition," complained Aisha.

Poor girl, thought Rose. She won't have much chance to be an individual and find out what she wants to do until Aisha stops trying to control and protect her. She asked, "Who was she with?"

"Francis Isaac, a minor government official at Meru County Council. They met at some function in Nairobi just before we left. At face value, he seems harmless enough. A little full of himself perhaps, but at least he looks after Pearl."

The name disturbed a memory. Rose had known an Isaac family in Timau, who'd run a small hardware shop. If she remembered correctly, there'd been a tragedy. The wife and a daughter had died because there had not been enough money to buy medicines.

Could this smartly dressed, and rather arrogant, young man be from the same family? If so, he had received more than his fair share of good fortune.

CHAPTER FOUR

Rose drove her old red Land Rover Defender the short distance home, feeling exhausted and numb. She had expected a cheerful chat with her childhood friend, Aisha, as they caught up on all that had happened since they'd last seen each other. But instead, she was sore from being shot at.

Home was a small, one-bedroom thatched cottage set in five acres of land. Rose kept a menagerie of animals including chickens, ducks, a cow, a horse, a dog and a one-eyed cat. Most of her animals had been given to her or rescued from neglectful owners.

She enjoyed working on the land and maintained a colourful garden at the front of the cottage. But she preferred working in her shamba at the back where she grew vegetables for the table, and herbs and flowers for her medicinal mixes.

Rose and her husband Craig had rented the house six years ago, when Craig retired from his farm manager's job. They decided it was time to settle in Nanyuki, with its shops and other facilities, the main one being the Cottage Hospital.

"Hello, dear. Have you had a pleasant afternoon?" Rose asked as she entered the living room. Craig was ensconced in his favourite high-backed chair, reading a book. Potto, her black and tan terrier, raced in from the bedroom and jumped up at her legs. She picked him up, but pushed his muzzle away as he tried to lick her face.

"Grand, thank you. The pain's been manageable and I watched racing from Scottsville in South Africa this afternoon. Dickie Chambers made an appearance earlier, and asked if I was happy to remain on the North Kenya Polo Club committee. He wanted to know if I'd consider putting my name forward for treasurer again."

Rose stroked Potto. "What did you tell him?"

"I said I'd be delighted to remain on the committee, but treasurer is too much for me these days, my health being what it is. I'm happy to assist and to do what I can."

"Fair enough. Is there anyone else on the committee from Nanyuki or will you need driving to meetings?"

Craig looked down at his book. "I told Dickie that with this gammy leg I wouldn't make them all. But I might need you to drive me to the important ones."

Instinctively, Rose looked across at Craig's left leg and his walking stick, which was propped against the arm of his chair. His childhood polio had paralysed his leg, but with enormous amounts of determination he'd learnt to ride and play polo.

Disturbingly, a version of the disease had resurfaced, causing muscle and joint weakness, together with pain and fatigue. Luckily, today he seemed relatively pain free.

Craig looked up at her. "You're very pale. Are you coming down with a bug? You must rest and stop doing so much. Now, if I had my way, you'd spend a bit less time gallivanting about and a bit more time sitting here keeping me company."

She lowered the wriggling Potto to the floor. "And do what? Knit? Besides, your pension only stretches so far, so we need to top it up with whatever payments I receive for my veterinary work, and the sale of my herbal mixes."

She picked up a dining chair, placed it opposite Craig, and sat down. With her hands clasped and resting on her knees, she looked at him and said, "I met Aisha Onyango today. I was rather surprised, especially as she shot me."

"She what?" Craig exclaimed.

"It's OK, just a graze." Rose lifted one side of the dressing on her arm, revealing an angry red line of damaged skin, surrounded by purple bruising. "I think she's frightened of something. She's moved her family up to Nanyuki and she's carrying a handgun for protection."

Craig tapped his fingers on the arm of his chair. "I know she used to be a close friend, and that she did us both a great service, but please keep away from her. She makes far more enemies than friends with her role on the EACC. And I don't want you getting mixed up in anything dangerous."

Rose clasped her hands together again. "Talking of the service she did for us. She told me she's looking into the incident at Ol Kilima, to see if it was connected with organised crime."

Craig scowled. "I don't understand. What's organised crime to do with it? And why open that can of worms again? I don't like this. I've a feeling in my bones that there's trouble ahead."

CHAPTER FIVE

R ose peered through the grimy windscreen of her battered Land Rover Defender. It was quarter to six on Friday morning, and traces of light emerged as she sped along the recently tarmacked road leading to Mount Kenya Resort and Spa. Threads of cloud, waiting to rise in the heat of a new day, further reduced visibility.

Julius, the head warden of the Mount Kenya Animal Orphanage, had summoned her only twenty minutes earlier, and she still wore her cotton nightie, tucked into her jeans, under her dark blue blouse.

Wincing, she grabbed the steering wheel, pulling swiftly into the middle of the road to avoid a group of five school children. They were barely visible in their blue uniforms, despite their red balaclava hats. Her hands and feet felt stiff, swollen and painful.

She had remembered to wear her grey fingerless compression gloves, which aided blood circulation, but her rheumatoid arthritis was always worse in the mornings. She wondered once again if she should stop early morning visits, but who else was there to assist Laikipia's animals?

Rose was not a qualified vet, but she had been stitching, injecting, and nursing a range of animals from elands to pet gerbils for over forty years. Despite recent legislation, she was allowed to continue her work and assist the local community under the authority of Nanyuki's only official vet, Dr Emma. Rose's title was Veterinary Paraprofessional, but to the local African community she was known simply as 'Mama Rose'.

Today's early morning emergency was a female bongo, a rare mountain antelope. It was in labour, but its calf was not presenting correctly. Both its front legs should extend forward, followed by the calf's head, so it appeared to be in a diving position, but Julius told her only one leg was visible.

Julius appeared wearing a green khaki uniform and peaked cap. He removed his clenched fist from his chin to greet Rose. "Asante, Mama Rose. I know it's an early start, but the bongo is not happy. Losing either the mother or calf would be a deep blow to us and our bongo recovery program."

Rose found the distressed bongo, with her reddish-brown hide and distinctive white stripes, rubbing against the timber posts of her pen. Changing position, the bongo scraped the earthen floor, bare except for a sprinkling of dried grass.

"Can you keep her still?" asked Rose. Another warden, a boy in his late teens, put his thin arm around the bongo's neck and, surprisingly, she stopped fidgeting.

"This is to make her relax. It stops her pushing too hard and damaging herself or her calf," Rose explained, administering an injection. Five minutes later the bongo stood comfortably. Rose exchanged her right glove for a latex one, which extended up her arm. It was time to get to work.

She flexed her painful fingers and braced herself. She pushed the calf back inside its mother, leaving her hand submerged. With considerable physical effort, she found and manoeuvred the second leg until both front legs were aligned and facing forward.

While she tied the calving ropes to each leg, she instructed the boy. "We need to help the bongo deliver this calf by pulling the front legs out. We must do it pole pole and carefully so as not to hurt the calf or its mother, sawa?"

The boy simply nodded and picked up a rope. Watching Rose, he anxiously mirrored her actions, and slowly but carefully, the calf was extracted from its mother onto the hard floor.

Rose stood, arching her back, as the boy confidently took over without needing further instructions. Walking out of the pen and peeling off the latex glove, Rose realised how weary she was from the physical effort of assisting the calf into the world. Her fingers ached, and the wound on her arm throbbed.

"Asante, Mama." A grateful Julius handed her a cup of hot chai. Despite the delicate morning sunshine, she shivered. There was often a chill in the air on the slopes of Mount Kenya.

"We will take great care of the calf," promised Julius.

"As long as you don't spoil it. This one needs to be released into the wild as it's imperative we raise the number of wild bongo to over a hundred, if they are to survive."

Julius bowed his head and replied, "Mama, your help with the breeding programme is greatly appreciated, and once again, you have come to our rescue. Asante."

CHAPTER SIX

R ose manoeuvred her old Land Rover into a tight parking space in front of 'I Love Nanyuki' Coffee Shop, known locally as Dormans. It faced a broken tarmac road running parallel with Kenyatta Avenue, the main highway running through Nanyuki. Squeezing herself out of the car, she looked around and noticed a black Land Cruiser parked across the street.

A crown of blonde hair was all that was visible as a gaggle of street traders engulfed the driver who emerged from the car. Their arms extended with objects ranging from wooden carvings and handmade cards to DVDs in cellophane covers.

A yellow-coated parking attendant was patiently waiting at the rear of the car, writing the registration number in a booklet of tickets. The attendant tore off a ticket and waved it in the face of the bemused driver who had extracted herself from the local salesmen.

Rose waited. It was clear the lady was new to Nanyuki and might be who she had come to meet. She was in her late thirties, tall and slim, with cascades of glossy blonde hair. She strode purposely across the road, wearing a smart knee-length pencil skirt, with a matching top and jacket, and large round sunglasses.

She stumbled as her heel caught in a crack in the road, and Rose thought she caught a low hissing curse.

Righting herself, the lady nearly knocked into Rose, but drew back at the last minute with a gasp.

"Are you Chloe?" Rose asked.

Patting down her hair and trying to straighten her skirt at the same time, the lady answered, "Are you Heather's mum?"

"Yes, Rose. Come on, let's find a table." The coffee shop occupied the left third of the building in front of them, but made use of the whole courtyard. A canopy extended from the building provided shade for some tables, whilst others had their own canvas umbrellas.

A metre-high concrete wall with a picket fence on top surrounded the courtyard. Green-leafed plants grew against the fence, providing customers a shield from local touts, and dust from the street. But particles of dust, thrown up by passing cars, still danced in the sunshine.

"Is this OK?" Rose asked, standing beside a rectangular picnic-style table with four attached seats.

"Lovely," Chloe responded limply, using a napkin from the table to wipe down a seat. She slid onto it, under the protection of the fence and plants, but wrinkled her nose and used the napkin to brush a splatter of dust off her jacket.

Rose apologised, "I'm afraid there's either dust in the dry season or mud in the rainy season, and not much in between."

A shadow fell across their table and Rose looked up at the shrewd, hooded eyes of a waiter twirling a small white pencil. "Habari, Daniel," she greeted the waiter. "Just a tea for me, please. Do you have any Kericho Gold?"

"Habari, Mama Rose. Yes, we do. And for you, madam?" he asked Chloe.

"A tall skinny latte with an extra shot please."

Daniel's pencil hovered over a notebook. "Sorry, what was that?"

Rose responded quickly. "A large latte. Do you have any semi-skimmed milk?"

"I asked for skimmed milk, and an extra shot. I need the caffeine," quipped Chloe.

"No skimmed milk, madam. Maybe semi-skimmed. I will check," answered Daniel.

"I would advise against an extra shot at this altitude," Rose cautioned.

"How complicated is it to get a coffee?" cried Chloe, ignoring the curious looks of other customers.

Daniel stepped back, raising his hand. "Pole madam, a large latte, extra shot, semi-skimmed milk if available. Anything to eat?"

"No, thank you. Just the coffee."

Oh dear, not a great start, thought Rose. Chloe looked less sophisticated now with her protruding eyes and ruffled hair.

"Why did you try to change my order?" Chloe asked, securing her sunglasses in her hair.

"I think Heather said you were living in London?" Rose asked, and Chloe nodded.

"It's rather different in Kenya. Many products you are used to in the UK aren't available here. Of course, Nairobi has a greater choice than Nanyuki, but we don't have skimmed milk, and semi-skimmed is only available when there has been a recent delivery. As for an extra shot of coffee, I've heard other ladies, new to the town, say too much caffeine makes them punch drunk. I guess it's because we are sitting at over six thousand feet above sea level. You won't have acclimatised yet so just be careful, as there may be times when you get short of breath."

At this, Chloe brightened. "Oh, I just presumed I was very unfit when I found running so hard this morning."

Rose smiled and added, "Why do you think Kenya has so many medal winning long distance and marathon runners? Living and training at high altitude gives them a significant advantage."

"So there might be some benefits to moving here," mused Chloe.

Rose cleared her throat and asked, "How did you meet my daughter?"

"In London, at an ex-British military event. She told me you lived here and that we should meet. And as I don't know anyone else, I called you." Looking carefully at Rose, Chloe took another napkin and handed it across. "You've spilt something on your shirt."

Rose looked down and answered levelly. "Thank you, it's probably fluid from the bongo calf I delivered earlier this morning. I didn't have time to change before meeting you." Chloe squealed and inwardly Rose grinned, remembering that she still had her nightie on underneath.

CHAPTER SEVEN

Rose was sitting at a table in the courtyard outside Dormans coffee shop. Opposite her was Chloe, a new arrival in Nanyuki.

Chloe sat up straighter. Rose followed her gaze as an attractive African couple entered from the street. She recognised her friend Aisha's daughter, Pearl, and her boyfriend, Francis. Francis' mouth was set in a hard line as he surveyed the other occupants and led Pearl to the table beside Rose and Chloe.

Pearl's cheeks flushed, and her face tightened as Francis' eyes roamed over Chloe. Chloe flicked her blonde hair and, reaching into her bag, retrieved and applied a fresh coat of lipstick.

Daniel materialised, placing Rose and Chloe's drinks on the wooden table. He spun toward the recent arrivals, but instead of stopping to take their order, he walked away. Intrigued, Rose turned her head and watched Daniel confer with a waitress, whilst pointing at Pearl and Francis, before he disappeared inside the coffee shop.

"How do I stop those people shoving things in my face when I get out of the car? And why was that lady waving a piece of paper at me repeating 'twenty bob, you have to pay twenty bob'?" Chloe asked, regaining Rose's attention.

"The lady wanted money for car parking. In the future, look for a space in front of here as parking is free for coffee shop customers." Rose poured milk into her tea and swirled it around with a spoon.

"The street hawkers see you as fair game, as you're an attractive, well-dressed white woman in an expensive car. They believe you can afford what they have to sell, even if you don't want it.

Just be firm. Put up your hand and say 'hapana', meaning no, and walk purposefully away."

Rose took a sip of tea before continuing. "They're just trying to make a living, but there's only so many beaded bracelets or wooden animals you'll want. Personally, I like the hand-painted cards and many people buy the DVDs."

Chloe rubbed her chin and confessed, "I'm also confused about money. What's the difference between Kenyan shillings and bob? And what's the exchange rate for UK pounds?"

Rose reached into her pocket but only found a thousand shilling note. She gestured to Chloe. "Show me what's in your purse and I'll try to explain."

Chloe reached into her leather tote bag and extracted a bulging purse. "It's like monopoly money," she proclaimed. "A thousand shilling note is the largest I can get, so I have a stack of them bundled into my wallet."

Rose reached across and covered the open wallet. "Be careful! People are always watching. You're carrying around the equivalent of a month's pay for most locals, so somebody might try to steal it.

Here, give me your purse," she gestured with her hand. "Bob is just slang for shillings."

She took a thousand shilling note out of Chloe's purse and held it up. "Use your phone to check what this is worth."

Chloe picked up her phone, tapped a few keys and said, "About seven pounds fifty."

Rose waved a two hundred shilling note and Chloe tapped more keys.

"That's about one pound fifty."

"If you like using your phone, you can also store and send money with it. Even non-technical people like me find it convenient, and much safer than carrying around wads of cash. It's called 'Mpesa'. M stands for mobile whilst pesa is Swahili for money, so it's literally mobile money. You can register at the Safaricom shop in the mall, but you'll need your passport for ID."

Rose tipped a handful of coins onto the table from Chloe's wallet. She separated them with her finger. "This small silver coin is one shilling and the slightly larger one two shillings."

Chloe frowned, picking up a battered bronze coloured coin. "But this also says one shilling."

"Yes, you'll find several older one shilling coins still in circulation, and sometimes fifty cent coins, which are pretty worthless." Rose manoeuvred coins around the table with her right index finger forming a line. "There, one to forty shillings in coins."

Whilst Chloe examined the money, Rose overheard part of the conversation from the adjacent table.

"Do I have to sit next to Governor Omolo? He's so… creepy. And his hands have a habit of wandering up my leg. It gets worse after a few drinks." Pearl shuddered.

Francis rested his arms squarely on the table, with his hands clenched, and replied, "I need his support. And I've seen the way he relaxes with you, especially after a few drinks. Besides, I've bought you that dress we saw in Nairobi, gold silk…"

"With the long slits up the legs. That'll be even more of an invitation for the Governor!" Pearl groaned.

Francis leaned back and ran his eyes up and down her. He said disparagingly, "Betty would be about your size and she told me last week that she would do anything I asked."

Thoughts visibly raced across Pearl's face and Rose's stomach clenched for the young girl, so attracted to this clever man who was manipulating her. Rose squeezed her hands, hoping Pearl would be strong.

"OK, I'll go," whispered Pearl.

Francis stood up, smugly throwing a thousand shilling note on the tabletop. He kissed Pearl on the forehead and said, "Come at six and change at mine. And don't say your Ma won't like that." He straightened the front of his jacket with both hands and left.

Rose looked quickly back at Chloe as Pearl began to look about dejectedly.

"What is there to do here apart from drinking coffee?" Chloe asked, looking around Dormans and frowning at what she saw. Rose realised many of the mid-morning coffee crowd were preparing to leave, so they could buy their groceries before meeting friends for lunch. She exchanged waves and greetings with some of them.

Returning to Chloe, she said, "These people might not dress in designer outfits, but they're hardworking, down to earth and enjoy a good party. It will take time for them to get to know you, and it's as if there are various clubs: farmers, Podo School mums, and safari camp managers. But they'll accept you with time, if you are prepared to become part of their world and do something for them, like join a committee or volunteer at an orphanage."

Chloe's eyes opened as wide as a startled wildebeest.

Rose rested a hand on her arm and said softly, "Don't worry, it may seem overwhelming now, but you'll soon settle in, and I'm sure you'll be invited to lots of parties. People in Nanyuki love fresh blood!".

Realising she'd used her last thousand shilling note to pay for the drinks, Rose strode up the street towards Barclays Bank. She had expected

Chloe to settle the bill, but the poor girl had fled Dormans without finishing her coffee.

Rose feared she was flinging designer dresses into large suitcases and phoning for a taxi to take her to Jomo Kenyatta International Airport, in Nairobi.

Rose heard a shriek of brakes and stopped abruptly. A boda-boda motorbike, ridden by two helmeted men, cut across her path and skidded to a halt. She hoped they didn't want money.

The rear figure removed his helmet as Rose held her breath. "Mmmama Rose!"

She laughed in relief. It was Thabiti.

"I scared you, pole. But Ma told me to find you and give you this." He held up a silver envelope as he dismounted the motorbike. "She's throwing a party tomorrow evening. I think she's trying to persuade herself everything's OK," he said, fumbling and dropping the envelope.

Picking it up, he pleaded, "Please come. She needs some support."

Returning to the boda-boda, he climbed on behind the driver and called, "See you tomorrow."

CHAPTER EIGHT

At half-past five on Saturday evening, Rose parked her battered Land Rover Defender in the rear yard of Guinea Fowl Cottage. She noticed with concern that there were hardly any other vehicles.

A white Land Cruiser and a green Rav 4 were protected from the harshness of the Kenyan sun by shade netting draped over a simple wooden frame.

A black Subaru Impreza was parked by the garden entrance and a white van with 'Avocado Catering' painted on the side was backed up to the gate leading to the rear of the cottage.

A figure emerged and carried a large silver platter into the house. At least preparations were underway for a party. But where were the other guests?

Rose felt a fluttering in her tummy. Something was not right. She slowly made her way through the garden to the front of the house, and as she climbed the steps to the veranda, she spotted Thabiti standing by a makeshift bar, staring at a sheet of paper. A large man stood behind him, polishing glasses.

Glasses! Rose thought, and her hand shot up to her mouth.

"Mama Rose, is everything OK?" called Thabiti.

"I'm early, aren't I? When you gave me the invitation, I didn't have my glasses on." Rose remembered standing in the street outside Barclays Bank. "And I must have read the wrong time."

Thabiti checked his watch. "The other guests aren't due for an hour, but are you happy to wait? And shall I tell Ma you're here? She's changing in the guest cottage."

"No need to bother her," Rose said as she climbed the remaining steps.

"You look nice," Thabiti said timidly.

Rose's cheeks flushed. How polite of Thabiti. She wore earrings and a little blusher, but that didn't hide her old trousers, which were a little too short and revealed her bony ankles. But she was proud of the flowery blouse she had recently purchased from a local market stall. The label stated Laura Ashley, which sounded very designer.

Thabiti fiddled with his piece of paper and asked, "Are you on your own?"

"Yes, Craig can't stand up for long periods. But when he sits down, he feels he's missing out and becomes frustrated and grumpy. I thought he'd be happier at home this evening."

Thabiti glanced up and then back at his paper. "I wish I could join him. I hate parties. Too many people. So don't expect to see me once it starts. Ma's put me in charge of the music, so hopefully I can hide away with my laptop. Now I must sort out the extra songs for tonight's playlist."

Thabiti turned away from Rose but swivelled back and asked, "Tea. Would you like Doris to bring you some?"

Rose settled herself on a wicker chair. She looked up as Pearl, wearing a pink striped kikoi dressing gown, breezed past her without saying a word and descended the veranda steps.

Rose was content to gaze upon the manicured garden. Although there had been no rain for three months, the lawn was a neat carpet of green kikuyu grass. The perimeter flower beds were filled with waving fronds of fountain grass, dangling purple, pink and white bells of fuchsias and the miniature suns of marigold flowers.

She jumped as she heard rattling and a thump. Turning, she saw the large man who had been polishing glasses, stack crates of Tusker beer and cases of wine beside the bar. He opened a large plastic cool box and poured ice into it.

Disturbed, she stood and walked down the steps into the garden, nearly tripping over a startled and squawking guinea fowl as it dashed out from under the veranda. From the bottom of the garden, she viewed Mount Kenya, which appeared to be brooding under an ominous blanket of cloud.

Rose shuddered, but hoped it signalled the imminent arrival of rain to break the murderous heat of the last few months.

Looking back at the house, she saw Francis leaning against the veranda rail, but he ignored her. He was watching a figure, wearing a bright red and green kanga skirt with a matching head turban, leave the guest cottage.

"Good evening, Aisha. I hope tonight's a success." The figure nodded and walked along the path to the back of the cottage.

Rose joined Francis on the veranda. He wore a shiny blue suit and matching tie with a large knot at the throat. Brazenly, he lifted his left cuff to check the time on his ostentatious gold watch.

Was he ignoring her on purpose?

"Francis, isn't it? Aisha introduced us a few days ago." She felt like a boran cow as he ran his cold eyes quickly, but efficiently, up and down her, pinching his mouth. She stiffened, but spotted the guinea fowl again, which was strutting around the lawn and it reminded her of this self-important man. She laughed, and Francis stepped back, nearly colliding with the barman.

Pearl rushed onto the veranda, adjusting her dress. "I can't fasten my zip. Can you help?" She stood with her back to Francis.

"Of course, Pearl. Everything OK?" he asked calmly.

Turning, she gulped. "Yes, all done."

Rose coughed, and they both jumped slightly before facing her. Pearl flushed and, slightly flustered, asked, "Are you one of Ma's friends? Were you here the other afternoon?"

"Yes, this is Rose. I think she's a local." Francis's tone was patronising.

Rose opened her mouth… and shut it. There was a shriek. The barman dropped the glass he was cleaning. It broke into a myriad of pieces, which flew across the wooden floor.

"Aargh!" shrieked Pearl, putting a hand on her ankle. She raised it and a small spot of blood glistened on her fingertip.

CHAPTER NINE

Rose was standing on the veranda of Guinea Fowl Cottage when she heard the scream. The large barman sped into the house, and Rose followed as quickly as she could.

Francis remained on the veranda, calming Pearl, who was fussing over the cut on her leg.

Rose rushed through the living-cum-dining room, into the kitchen and beyond it to the dhobi room. Two white-clad chefs scuffled in the open doorway as they both tried to peer out of the house.

There was a wailing noise, and then a cry. "No, mistress."

Doris, sobbing loudly, elbowed her way between the chefs. Her eyes were wild, her nostrils flared, and her skin was flushed. What had distressed her so much? She stopped in front of Rose, clutching herself, and said in a hoarse voice, "Mama, she's dead. What shall I do? My mistress is dead!" Doris stuffed her fist into her mouth, but a huge sob escaped and she rushed off.

"Let me through," Rose commanded, pushing past the barman and chefs. She stepped across the perimeter path and entered a mottled white tent. Daniel, the waiter from Dormans coffee shop, was rooted to the spot. She stepped past him and stared down at the dead body of her old friend, Aisha Onyango.

Rose covered her face with her hands, taking deep breaths. She had suspected something was worrying Aisha, and that all was not right, but she had not expected her friend to die. How had it happened?

Realising her eyes were closed, she unscrewed them, removed her hands and looked down at the body. She just managed to stop herself from looking away again as Aisha's vacant eyes stared back. They were menacing, surrounded by black eye sockets. Had someone punched her in both eyes? How odd. And although Aisha still wore her bright kanga skirt and white shirt, her kanga headscarf was missing.

Thabiti knelt beside his mother, wide eyed. His mouth hung open and his face was a pale pink.

Rose bent down, touching him lightly on the shoulder. "Thabiti." She shook him. "Thabiti." This time he turned to face her, so she asked, "Can you go outside and call the police?" She spoke gently, but firmly.

"Also, find the large barman and ask him to stand at the entrance gate. The party guests will be arriving soon and we need to turn them away. Tell him to say there's been an accident." Rose hoped she was right, that it was an accident.

CHAPTER TEN

Rose was sitting on a wicker chair on the veranda of Guinea Fowl Cottage. It seemed like hours since she'd heard a shriek alerting her to the death of her friend, Aisha Onyango, but it had happened only an hour ago. Instead of tea, she sipped a gin and tonic but reeled as the gin burned her throat and tingled her lips. There could only be a splash of tonic in it.

Pouring out of the house came Thabiti, Pearl, Francis, Doris, and Daniel, the waiter, with the large barman and the two chefs Rose had seen earlier. Herding them was an elderly man in an impressive dark blue uniform, with a row of twisted silver oak leaves decorating his peaked cap. This was Police Commissioner Akida in his best uniform.

Pearl and Francis sat together on the small wicker sofa. Thabiti offered the other chair to Doris, but she refused, preferring to lean against the wooden balustrade with the other staff. Thabiti sat down but was sweating and squeezing his hands together with his knees.

Commissioner Akida stood opposite them. "Terrible business, just terrible," he said, wringing his hands. "I was on my way here when I received the call that a dead body had been discovered." He stood up straighter and became businesslike, but his fingers continued to fidget. "I have examined the body and can confirm it is my old friend and former colleague, Aisha Onyango."

He looked down at his shiny black shoes, shook himself, and continued. "There is a dent at the base of her skull from striking, or being struck by, a blunt object. From her panda eyes, which remind me of some car crash victims, I would say she suffered a basilar fracture."

So Aisha had not been punched in the face. If she had fallen back and hit her head, would the pressure have been enough to cause such secondary injuries to her eyes?

The commissioner answered Rose's unspoken question. "She could have fallen against something, but I only found trestle tables, crates and serving platters. It is unlikely that any of these would have provided sufficient force to cause such injuries. So I conclude that there has been foul play, and that Aisha Onyango was murdered."

There were gasps and cries from the assembled group, but Rose also thought she heard a deep sigh of self-congratulation.

Commissioner Akida continued, "One of my officers has taken over at the gate to turn away late arrivals for the party. Thank you, Mama Rose, for your quick thinking in organising that earlier. We are still telling everyone there has been an accident. For now, I need a brief statement from each of you, accounting for your actions and observations this afternoon and evening. I hope the process won't take too long, so you can return to your respective homes."

He patted his jacket and found a pen, but still looked around helplessly.

Rose called to Thabiti, but he refused to look at her. "Thabiti," she said again. This time, his head jerked up. "Can you get something, paper or a notebook, so I can write notes for the commissioner?"

As if waking from a trance, Thabiti staggered upright and weaved his way into the house. After a few minutes of strained silence, broken by the occasional forlorn cough and shuffling of feet, a more composed Thabiti returned. He handed Rose a small red notebook and blue biro.

"Carry on, Commissioner," instructed Rose.

The commissioner focused on Rose. "Well... where was I? Yes." The commissioner spied the house girl. "Doris, is it? I will start with you and then perhaps you can make some tea and coffee?" Doris looked like a small grey mouse stuck in a trap; she even squeaked when the commissioner addressed her. He continued gently, "Can you tell me what you were doing this afternoon, up until the time your mistress's body was found?"

Doris began in a shrill voice. "It's horrid. I spend today cleaning and tidying. Mistress want everything right for the party." She glanced in Pearl's direction, but the girl ignored her, playing instead with one of her silver and pearl earrings. "I finish all my jobs, and just sit down in the dhobi room, to rest my poor feet and drink a cup of chai, when a white van parks in the yard. It is these men."

She pointed at the chefs, Daniel, the waiter, and the large barman. "So, I gets up again and show them where to put things. I finish my chai and they carry lots of crates and boxes to the house and tent."

"When was the tent erected?" asked the commissioner.

"Some men come this morning. Dirty." Doris wrinkled her nose. "I give it good flick flick with my brush to get rid of dirt and dust."

"So when you had finished your chai?" The commissioner pushed up on the soles of his shoes.

"I iron a skirt for Miss Pearl. I take it to her room with a cup of tea, but that man bump into me." She pointed towards the smaller of the two white-clad chefs whose oval face and dark eyes remained impassive. "Oh, dear." She faltered, but with an encouraging nod from the commissioner, continued her account.

"The tea, it splash on me, leave small brown patches. Lucky none land on the skirt but I not work with dirty uniform. I change in my room and put on clean uniform." She picked at the hem of her dress.

"Did you see anything unusual?" The commissioner swayed back and forth.

Putting her head to one side, she appeared to consider the question. "No, sir, nothing unusual. No one who should not be there. Then I help that nice young man chop vegetables. Master Thabiti say Mama Rose is early for the party. I knows she like tea so I take a cup out to her." She gave Rose a crooked smile.

"Thank you, Doris," said the commissioner, and she scampered off towards the house. Rose noticed her hands were trembling.

Commissioner Akida turned towards the two bald, white-clad chefs. The one on the left was tall, with a large domed head, gold earring and amiable demeanour. By contrast, his colleague was shorter, older, and had a full black beard and pencil moustache. Rose shivered. She would not like to encounter him in a Nanyuki back street at dusk.

The older man spoke. "Our job was in the kitchen, preparing food for the guests, and that is where we stayed."

"Except when you bumped into Doris?" commented Rose.

"Good point," nodded the commissioner.

"I was lost." The chef shrugged nonchalantly.

"I visited the tent to fetch equipment," added the younger man helpfully.

Neither offered any further information. Rose scrutinised them both. The younger man looked as if there was nothing else he could tell the commissioner, but the older chef was agitated, avoiding eye contact, and he shifted his weight from side to side. Rose pursed her lips. Just what was he hiding?

CHAPTER ELEVEN

Commissioner Akida stood on the veranda of Guinea Fowl Cottage and studied the people assembled before him. He turned to Daniel, the waiter, and said, "Daniel, I understand you found the body."

Daniel nodded.

"Then I'll question you later. Who is the big man beside you?"

"I'm Sam, the barman," the bear of a man growled with his hands in his pockets.

"Are you new to the area? I have not seen you before." Commissioner Akida leaned forward.

Sam smiled, and Rose thought he looked like a large cat toying with a mouse. "No, we haven't met."

The commissioner rubbed his chin and asked, "So your movements were?"

"I arrived in the van, as the maid said. She told me the lady of the house wanted the bar set up over there." He extended his arm towards the makeshift bar. "I put up the trestle tables, sorted out my equipment and cleaned some glasses."

"And did you see the 'lady of the house'?"

"Yes, she spoke to me as I was putting up the tables and I had confirmed to her that I had brought the ingredients and equipment to make mojito cocktails. She examined the wine and left."

The commissioner looked at him quizzically. "And that was the last you saw of her?"

"Actually, no. Later this gentleman greeted her as she walked past the side of the house." He pointed towards Francis.

The commissioner laced his fingers together. "I may have more questions for you. Please give

Mama Rose your current address and mobile number so I can contact you if I need to."

Sam walked forward, squatted on his haunches, and gave Rose the requested information, which she wrote in the red notebook.

Doris appeared carrying cups on a large round green tray with a guinea fowl painted on it.

Sam returned to the back of the group and leaned nonchalantly against the veranda rail, his arms crossed.

The commissioner appeared about to speak when Doris bustled out again, dumping pots of tea and coffee on the table. Some coffee sloshed out, making Doris gasp. She put her hand to her mouth and rushed back into the house.

Ignoring the drinks, Commissioner Akida turned to Francis. "And what is your connection with the Onyango family?"

Puffing out his chest and sitting up straighter, Francis replied, "I'm an officer with the Meru County Government." He paused, seeming to expect a reaction from the commissioner, but instead his statement was met with silence and a blank look.

Rose looked down and felt herself giggle. She coughed, hoping she'd hidden it. Ignoring her, Francis removed a small gold box from the inside pocket of his suit jacket and extracted a gold-edged business card, which he handed to the commissioner. "I am Pearl's partner." Pearl looked startled—maybe this was a revelation to her.

"And your name, sir?" the commissioner asked.

"As you can see from my official card, Francis Isaac." Francis brushed the collar of his jacket.

"Thank you." The commissioner pocketed the business card. "And what were your movements this afternoon?"

"I drove down from my office in Meru and freshened up in Pearl's room. I came out onto the veranda around six o'clock and I saw this woman walking in the garden." He gestured towards Rose without looking at her.

Commissioner Akida looked at Rose, who nodded in agreement. "Did you see or speak with Mrs Onyango?"

"Yes, I saw her from the veranda when she emerged from her cottage. But she only waved and walked along the path to the back of the house."

Looking around at the group, the commissioner said, "I still need to speak with Daniel, Pearl and Thabiti, but the rest of you may leave."

Addressing Rose, he said, "Would you mind staying to continue note-taking?"

Rose had promised Craig she would be home early as he'd been complaining again that she was too involved in community activities. What would he make of her being caught up in a murder?

She replied, "Could you send an officer to my house to tell Craig what's happened? And reassure him that I'm all right and will be home soon." Commissioner Akida left in search of a policeman. The barman and chefs followed him.

"Mama Rose, tea?" Thabiti asked with a shaking hand on the teapot.

"Please." She pushed away the glass of gin she had barely touched.

Commissioner Akida returned and announced, "I have sent Constable Wachira to see Craig. Mr Isaac, please leave, or at least go into the house."

Francis seemed about to protest but hesitated, squeezed Pearl's hand, and taking his coffee, he walked into the house.

CHAPTER TWELVE

R ose remained on the veranda of Guinea
Fowl Cottage with Commissioner Akida,
Pearl, Thabiti and Daniel, the waiter.

The commissioner addressed Daniel. "Please tell
me how you discovered the body?"

Daniel ran his tongue along his lips. "It's nothing
to do with me. I always get the blame, but I didn't
do it." His voice rose to a shout. The
commissioner looked flustered by Daniel's
unexpected outburst.

"Calm down, Daniel," Rose commanded. "No
one's accusing you of anything. Just tell the
commissioner what happened."

"I saw the mistress of the house on the floor of the tent. She was dead. And her eyes stared right through me." He shuddered. "She hadn't been there ten minutes earlier."

Rose looked at him sharply and asked, "How do you know?"

"I was in and out of that tent all afternoon. 'Fetch this, Daniel... take that.' The chefs like ordering me about. When I collected cutlery ten minutes earlier, she wasn't there, I tell you. I only went back to fetch the napkins." Daniel wrinkled his brow and looked away.

"What did you do when you found the body?" asked the commissioner.

"Do? Oh, I think I screamed or shouted. Doris grabbed my arm, babbling in Swahili. Master Thabiti arrived and then Mama Rose took control."

"Did you see Mrs Onyango alive at any point during the afternoon?" asked the commissioner.

"Yes, she was around, ordering people about, and checking up on things."

"Can you be more specific?" The commissioner wriggled his fingers.

Daniel rubbed his nose. "I saw her out here when I carried equipment from the van. She was talking to Sam."

"And that was all?"

"Yes." Daniel looked down at his feet.

Liar, thought Rose.

"OK, Daniel. Give your details to Rose. I will definitely need to talk to you again."

Daniel turned to Thabiti. "Can I have two hundred shillings for a boda-boda home? The others will have left without me."

Thabiti looked up at Daniel. He quickly dropped his head, fumbled in his pocket and extracted a few crumpled notes, which he handed to Daniel without looking up. Daniel grunted his thanks and left.

"Thabiti," the commissioner said.

Thabiti looked up and said, "I'm happy to tell you what I did, but can you wait until tomorrow to question Pearl?"

"Please don't treat me any differently." Pearl said in a hollow voice. "I'd rather give my account now."

"OK, Pearl. What can you tell me?" The commissioner leaned against Rose's chair.

"I spent most of the afternoon in my room. Francis joined me and changed for the party. I think Thabiti had just gone out when I went to the kitchen to ask Doris for tea. I wondered why she took her time—she had spilt the first cup. I went to see Ma sometime between half five and six o'clock and then returned to my room to change. That's all."

In a quieter tone than usual, the commissioner said, "Thank you. If you remember anything else, please tell me. Once the shock has worn off you may see things slightly differently."

Thabiti spoke slowly and deliberately. "I spent most of my time in town sorting out party stuff. Between trips, I spoke to Ma. That must have been around quarter past four, as the caterers had arrived and she was talking to the barman. She seemed a little preoccupied, but I assumed it was from organising the party. I had to go out for more ice and didn't see her again, although I heard Francis greet her as I got into the shower."

Rose felt an ache in her throat for Thabiti, who, despite his young age and apparent anxiety, was acting in a very restrained manner.

"Thank you, Thabiti, for your direct and succinct account." The commissioner addressed Pearl and Thabiti. "These interviews may seem callous at this distressing time, but it is imperative I establish a timeline, whilst the evening's events are fresh in everyone's minds."

He clasped his hands in front of him, then dropped them back to his side. "You have my deepest sympathy. Although I had not seen your mother for many years, we worked together in the past and I had the utmost respect for her, her honesty, and her values. Not everyone did. I think that will do for this evening. Thabiti, may I speak with you?" He gestured with his head, and they walked to the corner of the veranda. Rose could hear them murmuring.

"I'm so done. Goodnight," Pearl said as she left.

Without thinking, Rose tore a page from the notebook. She flicked through the notes she'd made, copying the most important details, including the addresses and phone numbers she had been given.

The men returned. "Thank you so much, Mama Rose. I apologise for keeping you here for so long. I have not taken your account of the evening, but perhaps that can wait until tomorrow."

"But tomorrow's Sunday, commissioner," Rose pointed out.

"So it is, but after tonight's events, I will have to go to the office. Are you attending church in the morning?" Rose nodded. "Would you mind visiting me at the station afterwards? It is just across the road from the catholic church and I can offer you coffee?"

"Of course, Commissioner, but I prefer tea."

Thabiti walked Rose to her car. The air was still except for the beat of crickets grinding their wings together. "Are you OK driving home?" he asked.

"Don't worry about me. You have enough to think about at the moment." She looked directly at him and said, "I'm always ready to listen should you need to talk."

Raised voices reached them, and they turned in the direction of the house. Pearl shouted, and a door slammed, reverberating in the silence. Out of the corner of her eye, Rose caught a movement. Then all was still.

CHAPTER THIRTEEN

On Sunday morning Rose attended the morning service at Christ the King Catholic Church, Nanyuki. She remained in her pew, with her head bowed, after other members of the congregation departed. She reflected on Aisha's death, and her feelings about it.

Craig had been most concerned about the effect on her rather than poor Aisha. In his own way, he was trying to be supportive, reminding her that Aisha actively sought involvement in commissions and legal cases, particularly those involving practices she disagreed with.

He also accepted there had to be more to her return to Nanyuki than Thabiti's issues at university, and that perhaps she had ruffled too many feathers.

Rose had slept fitfully and after waking from a nightmare at four in the morning, she could not return to sleep. In her dream, she and Aisha had been arguing about reopening old cases whilst grappling with a shotgun. When the gun fired, Rose found herself holding it and Aisha lying on the floor, a bloody hole in her chest.

Rose had woken suddenly, disorientated, with a woman's voice screaming in her head. She had screwed her eyes closed, but could still hear the echoes of that scream. Her stomach ached. She felt sad about Aisha, but also rather detached. Surely she should be crying, racked with sobs for a friend she had spent so much of her school years and early adulthood with.

She inhaled deeply and slowly. Of course, to her the body was not that of her former classmate, but of an older woman, scarred with the traumas of life. They had drifted apart forty years ago.

Rose bit her lip guiltily, as she also felt relief. Relief that Aisha would no longer investigate the incident. Relief that she would not reawaken old memories. Rose's demons were her own, to remain hidden from view. To the outside world, she would remain Mama Rose.

She flinched as a hand touched her shoulder. She looked up into the unusually stern face of Father Matthew. His gaze was direct, but his eyes were soft and questioning.

"Rose, why do you contain your grief? Why not share your pain with me? The Lord is merciful, and through him is the path to redemption."

"Father, I'm not ready. Mine is a burden too grave for salvation. It is one I must carry alone."

CHAPTER FOURTEEN

Outside Christ the King Catholic Church, the sounds, smells and sights of a typical Sunday in Nanyuki invaded Rose's introspection. Most African people attended church, which was more than could be said for their European neighbours.

She could hear the calls and chants of congregations from many religious denominations, and she visualised the bright dresses of the women and children.

Unlike her own sturdy stone Catholic Church, many places of worship were tin sheds, or simply ripped and stained tents. Congregations often sat on the floor or on unstable white plastic chairs.

Rose left her trusty Defender in the church car park and walked across the road to the police station for her meeting with Commissioner Akida. A white Toyota Probox swerved off the road ahead of her, sending a fountain of dust into the air as it braked to a stop.

Proboxes were inexpensive, small utility estate-style cars, favoured by many Africans for their ability to carry large numbers of people or produce, or both. Rose counted nine people peel themselves out of the boot of the car and smiled as they strolled away, chatting loudly in their ill-fitting suits and shiny dresses.

She entered the police compound and stepped over broken tarmac as she made her way around a single storey brick building. It was the original police headquarters, but now served only an administrative purpose.

She passed broken bottles and the wrecks of abandoned cars, with missing wheels and fractured windscreens, as she headed towards the commissioner's office. It was a modest brick building squeezed between several prefabricated tin structures.

Rose walked through an anteroom with a tidy desk and line of dented, grubby, sandy-coloured filing cabinets. Her knock on the open door was met with silence and, peering inside, she saw that the room was empty.

A chipped cup containing a dirty brown liquid remained on the desk. She sat down in the anteroom on one of three wooden chairs covered with frayed burgundy-fabric seats.

More prefabricated buildings had been erected opposite and from one of these she heard raised male voices. They were arguing about whose fault it was a car had backed into a pickup. Still no sign of the commissioner.

The argument ceased as a female voice made it plain that both drivers were inept and perhaps she should send them both to court. In the silence that followed, the commissioner appeared.

Despite it being a Sunday, he wore his uniform. It was not the dark blue of the previous evening, but khaki, with an open-necked shirt which was partially untucked. The commissioner rubbed a hand through his hair and looked up to see Rose waiting.

"Mama Rose, my apologies. I had completely forgotten about your visit as events have overtaken us."

Rose jumped up. "You mean you found the killer?"

He sighed and walked into his office. "Not exactly. I received a phone call from the Deputy Inspector General's Office this morning. I had been expecting such a call, and anticipated that officers would be sent from Nairobi to take over this case. You know that Aisha was well connected?"

Absentmindedly, the commissioner boiled a kettle, tipped the remnants of his cup into a surprisingly vibrant potted fern, and performed the ritual of tea making.

"Sugar?" he asked.

Rose declined.

The commissioner heaped three spoons of sugar into his cup, seemingly transfixed by the swirls as he stirred the liquid. "I have been ordered to drop the investigation and record it as an accidental death. Case closed." Finally, he regarded Rose, raising his eyebrows.

"Oh. That's unexpected." Rose was unsure how to respond.

"Unexpected? It is ridiculous!" He slammed his fist down on his desk. Tea slopped onto a stack of papers. He fussed about clearing up the mess. When he finally sat down, pulling straight the collar of his shirt, he stated, "It is very frustrating. But that's not your fault."

"Did they give a reason?" asked Rose.

"Officially, Aisha's latest investigation was very sensitive, involving practices which the government does not want to be made public."

"Meaning there are those with activities to hide."

"Exactly."

They both sat back in their chairs. Rose took a gulp of tea and immediately regretted her action. She coughed to cover up spitting most of it back into the cup. Was that metallic dust settling on the top? The commissioner raised a dull brown hanky, which she refused.

"Mama Rose, I wish to thank you for your help writing notes last night. Aisha was an old friend, although I had not seen her since she left Nanyuki in… it must have been 2003. The children were still young cubs. Since she settled in Nairobi, I had not spoken to her, and the first I knew of her return was when I received an invitation to her party."

The commissioner removed a penknife from his pocket and spun it around his fingers.

Rose said, "I won't divulge how we met again, but her story, that she left Nairobi because Thabiti was having problems at university, doesn't ring true. I also think she had concerns about a current case, concerns serious enough to send her running to Nanyuki. The trouble is, she wouldn't give me any details, as she probably believed it was safer that way."

"It appears she may have been right, particularly after last night." The commissioner prised open the blades in his penknife.

"But someone did kill her. You can't just close the case without finding out who and why. What about Pearl and Thabiti? Surely they need answers?" urged Rose.

"Do they? Would it not be easier if I recorded it as an accidental death? Then everyone can move forward."

Rose shook her head. "But that's not how it works. Pearl and Thabiti need answers so they can grieve."

"Well, I am afraid my hands are tied. I am an ageing lion and there are plenty of ambitious young men and women who want to be the alpha male. If I step out of line, it could be the excuse they need to force me into early retirement. But you, Rose," he said, looking at her intensely.

"Me what? I'm no lion, rather I see myself as a small bush baby."

"Why? Do you urinate on your hands and feet to give you a better grip on trees?"

"Ugh, I didn't realise they did that!" Rose sat on her hands.

"Cute they might be, hiding in trees at night with their large moon-eyes, but they are agile and expert hunters. They have excellent vision to seek prey and silently pounce on it."

"I hope you are not expecting me to pounce on any vermin?" This conversation was getting out of hand, but the commissioner appeared to be enjoying himself.

"No, just use your powers of observation to find the snakes, and I will be happy to do the rest. Bush babies also have acute hearing, which is a powerful asset in any investigation. Besides, you are respected by both the African and European communities, within which you will need to hunt for information."

Rose needed to put a stop to this line of thought. "Hunting is for the younger, fitter members of the tribe, not the wizened old females. Commissioner, I'm flattered you think me capable of investigating such a serious crime. But there's no escaping that I'm an ailing old woman with arthritis and a history of high blood pressure. I've no political affiliations or influential relatives. If someone is prepared to kill Aisha, then they wouldn't hesitate at harming Craig or myself. And we'd be defenceless. Then it would be our deaths you'd be investigating next."

The commissioner sighed. Whilst his attendance at church was sporadic, apparently he still remembered his Bible lessons, as he quoted: "So whoever knows the right thing to do and fails to do it, for him it is sin."

CHAPTER FIFTEEN

It was midday on Sunday by the time Rose pushed open the kitchen door at the rear of her cottage.

The commissioner's quote from the Bible had shaken her. She guessed it was from the Book of James, and she felt nauseous at the thought of blatantly committing a sinful act.

Kipto, Rose's house girl of indeterminate age, was scrubbing home-grown carrots in a worn and chipped Belfast sink. Over thirty years ago, Rose had found Kipto asleep in her barn, heavily pregnant and with a toddler beside her. She'd given her a job helping in the house and garden and Kipto had stayed with her, even when her children had moved away to jobs Rose found them. Kipto spoke very little Swahili or English, but instead conversed in her tribal tongue.

"Chamgei, Mama. Lunch be ready in an hour."

"Thank you, Kipto. Where's Craig?"

"Outside with his paper puzzle."

That was a relief. He'd been occupied with the crossword puzzle all morning.

"Can I have a cup of tea? I'll sit outside with him." She looked forward to a fresh cup of Kericho Gold tea to expel the metallic taste of the commissioner's brew.

She stepped out onto a covered patio at the front of the house. It boasted a magnificent view of Mount Kenya, the summit of which was clear of cloud this morning, so the entire mountain was visible.

There were two large cedar chairs, with comfy kikoi-covered cushions, and a matching three-seater sofa, which was really the size of a single bed. The garden displayed a neat bed of yellow and red alstroemerias and white alyssum, and violet periwinkles bordered the patio.

A small stone bird table stood under a red bottlebrush tree. Kipto left scraps on it each day and Rose loved to watch the birds gather and peck at their favourite morsels. Today there were a couple of superb starlings with rust-coloured tummies. Their iridescent blue backs and wings fascinated Rose as the light caught them, like oil on water.

"Hello, dear," said Rose, as she bent down and pecked Craig on his forehead. Picking his glasses off his head, she used them to study the crossword he was completing. "Five across, behaving ethically. Five letters."

"Moral. How was Father Matthew this morning?" said Craig, returning his glasses to his own head.

"A little on the fire and brimstone side," she replied, slumping onto the wooden sofa, and disturbing Izzy, her one-eyed black and white rescue cat, and Potto, her terrier. They both yawned before resuming their sleeping positions. Kipto appeared with Rose's tea and left silently.

"He quoted from Galatians. 'And let us not grow weary of doing good, for in due season we will reap, if we do not give up.'" Rose sat up straighter. "I'm sure he was directing the next quote at me when he said, 'Even in old age they will still produce fruit, they will remain vital and green.'"

"If he was referring to people using their time productively, he probably did. But you're always volunteering, and it's time others stepped up to the mark."

"I thought he was reading my mind." Rose frowned.

"He may be a man of God, but I doubt he can work that miracle." In a lower voice Craig mumbled, "I certainly can't."

"I heard that," retorted Rose, without looking up from her tea.

"Yes, dear. Anyway, why would you consider him a mind reader?"

Rose looked up and stared across at Mount Kenya. "Well, before the service, I went over yesterday evening's events. I was there, at the house, when someone killed Aisha. I should have been able to stop it but I did nothing. What did I miss? Why couldn't I save her?"

Potto repositioned himself on Rose's lap. As she hugged him, she felt tears begin to flow, and with them a release of tension she was unaware she'd been carrying around all day.

Craig rested his hands on his crossword puzzle and said, "Rose, don't blame yourself. You can't save everyone and everything."

"I can try," she muttered from inside the terrier's warm coat.

"Was there an intruder? Or was anyone acting strangely?" Craig asked.

"Not that I could tell. The only person who appeared at all flustered was Aisha's daughter, Pearl, when she was struggling with the zip of her dress."

Craig smoothed out the crossword. "There you are then. There's no point worrying or getting upset. And there's nothing you could have done. Did Kipto say when lunch would be ready?"

Rose ignored Craig's question. She rubbed her remaining tears away with the back of her hand and viewed the starlings flapping their wings on the bird feeder.

"I've just had a disturbing meeting with Commissioner Akida. He's been told to sweep the whole investigation under the carpet, as someone in Nairobi is worried about what might be uncovered." Rose fidgeted like a young girl in her seat. "He asked me to help him find out who killed Aisha."

The muscles in Craig's faced tensed. "Now, Rose, I hope you told him that was not on the agenda. You are not a born-again Miss Marple."

Rose laughed at the image which popped into her head. "Can you imagine me with a little straw hat, neat woollen suit, and one of those large leather handbags? I could listen to people's conversations over the garden hedge."

"Don't be ridiculous. The only conversations from the other side of our hedge are our neighbours discussing the price of potatoes or maize at market."

Rose slumped.

Craig continued softly, "You can understand my point, though. Aisha was murdered. And her work clearly involved people in Nairobi with the power to halt police investigations. They will hardly allow an old lady in Nanyuki to upset the status quo."

Rose was about to speak, but Craig raised his hand. "I know, you're worried about her children. But I'm sure they have friends and family in Nairobi to support them. Now leave it."

There was little point in continuing the discussion, as it would only make Craig angry. She knew he just wanted a quiet retirement, with no unsettling events to disturb it.

"Seven down," said Craig. "Four letters: love, honour and...?"

CHAPTER SIXTEEN

Mid-morning on Sunday, Thabiti woke up at Guinea Fowl Cottage feeling disoriented. It took several seconds for reality to take hold. He was in Nanyuki. He was alone. Ma was dead. Murdered!

He pulled a pillow over his face, blocking out the light. But hiding from the real world was not so simple. Perhaps he was wrong and he'd only been dreaming. He padded into the dining room, where discarded preparations for a party were evident. It was the same in the kitchen. At the sight of half-prepared food his stomach lurched and he only just reached the bathroom in time.

"Thabiti, are you OK?" called Pearl.

"I think so." He replied hoarsely. "What about you?"

"It's too early. I can't face the world yet. I'm going back to sleep."

"Is Francis here?" Thabiti enquired.

"No, I think he stayed with friends in town. Now please let me sleep."

Thabiti needed some fresh air, so he wandered out onto the veranda. He picked up a bottle of coke from the temporary bar and snuggled into a foetal position on the wicker sofa. Was Ma still here? He daren't look.

Commissioner Akida had said he would arrange for the mortuary to send a vehicle this morning to collect her. Poor Ma, lying outside all night. At least Doris had covered her with a shuka blanket.

A dishevelled and puffy-eyed Doris shuffled onto the veranda.

"Ambulance here. But I not work today." Abruptly, she left.

He couldn't really blame her. He didn't feel like doing anything, but what was an ambulance doing?

He shrank back against the sofa as two men dressed in hospital whites climbed the veranda steps. "Where's the body?" one man asked curtly.

"Have some respect for our loss." Thabiti briefly forgot himself, responding in kind. "She's lying in the tent at the side of the cottage. Where are you taking her?"

"To the Community Hospital. It'll cost three thousand five hundred shillings for collection and transport, six hundred shillings a day for storage, and five hundred shillings per visit."

Thabiti threw his coke bottle in fury, but the man ducked and ran off, shouting, "Payable before collection of the body."

No wonder the man dealt with dead bodies. It was surprising he hadn't become one of them. Thabiti could hear the guinea fowl scratching at the broken bottle shards. More mess to clean up... later.

Thabiti regained consciousness around midday, disturbed by a yapping dog. But they didn't have a dog. He heard a woman call from somewhere in the house. "Thabiti, Pearl."

He heard Pearl shout out, "Please leave us in peace."

"Are you OK?" the disembodied voice called again.

With a sigh, Thabiti pulled himself out of bed. He found an African lady, probably in her mid-thirties, placing a metal sufuria cooking pot on the kitchen worktop.

Thabiti's mouth hung open at such an unexpected sight. She was petite in build, but everything else about her was large: her full afro-style hair, large round yellow glasses and rich full voice.

"There you are. You must be Thabiti. I'm Dr Emma. I heard about your tragedy and reckoned you might need some wholesome food." At the mention of food, Thabiti's insides turned, but he managed to suppress the need to throw up again.

"Oh dear, you're very pale." Dr Emma peered at him.

He leant against a kitchen cupboard. "I'm OK," he stammered. "Thank you, though I doubt I can eat anything yet." Losing his battle, he rushed to the loo.

Returning five minutes later, he found the kettle boiling, and the kitchen cleared of party food. A bulging black bin bag was propped beside the door.

"Doctors' orders, something hot and sweet to drink. I'm not a real doctor, though. I treat animals."

"Like Mama Rose."

Dr Emma beamed. "You know Mama Rose."

"She was here last night… when it happened."

There was a scratching at the dhobi room door. "I'd forgotten about her." Dr Emma opened the door and a white bundle of fluff yelped and spun in circles, before sniffling at the bin bag. "I thought you might like a dog. She'll keep you company."

"What? No thanks. I've enough trouble looking after myself."

"Caring for someone, or something else, can help the mourning process. And she's also grieving. Her owners abandoned her in their house when they left Nanyuki. Neighbours heard her barking, and I had to break in to rescue her. I've been feeding her, and all her jabs are up to date, so now she just needs someone to love her."

Thabiti looked down and found the little dog staring back at him. She yapped and thumped her tail. "Does she understand we're talking about her?"

Thabiti automatically took the mug Dr Emma offered. Warmth spread through him as he sipped the sweet tea and his tummy settled. "I'll call her Pixel."

There was a shout from the veranda and Commissioner Akida strode in.

"Commissioner," nodded Dr Emma. "My cue to leave. I've left some dog food in the dhobi room to get you started and I'll look in on you both in a few days."

Thabiti realised he was standing before the commissioner wearing only a T-shirt and boxer shorts.

"Do you mind if I change?" he asked, hugging his body.

"No problem. Have a shower, freshen up. I'm not in a hurry," responded the commissioner.

Pixel accompanied Thabiti to his room, making a nest for herself in his crumpled duvet.

Taking the commissioner at his word, Thabiti soaked his body for a long time in steaming hot water, until it ran out. Pearl wouldn't be happy, as she'd have to wait for the sun to heat up more water before she could shower.

He found the commissioner sitting at the cedar dining table on the veranda, leafing through a Laikipia Wildlife magazine, with a vulture guinea fowl on the front cover. Commissioner Akida appraised him for several minutes, during which time he felt increasingly uncomfortable and shuffled on the wooden bench.

The commissioner began, "There is no easy way to tell you this, so I will get straight to the point. The investigation into your mother's death has been halted, and I've been ordered to record it as an accidental death."

Thabiti shook his head, trying to clear his ears. Had he heard correctly? His mother's case was to be closed?

"What? Just like that? No questions? No suspects?"

The commissioner spread his fingers out on the table. "Your mother would understand. She knew the way the system works, politics, and all that…" the commissioner's voice trailed off.

"She knew, and fought it all her life. No, this is not how it will be."

The commissioner tapped the table. "Now, Thabiti, I know you are angry and upset, but I have my orders. They come directly from the Deputy Inspector General's Office. So there is nothing more I can do."

Thabiti felt his mouth open and shut like a wooden puppet. He couldn't make a sound. Finally, he managed to speak. "Let me get this right. My mother, a government employee, a respected lawyer, an advocate for equality in Kenya, for justice for all, is to be denied her own justice."

Hanging his head and shuffling his feet, the commissioner responded simply, "Yes."

A heavy silence hung between them.

Clasping his hands together, the commissioner looked up and said, "I have a suggestion, although as I have tried and failed, I doubt it will work."

"Go on," growled Thabiti.

"You could ask Mama Rose to help you investigate. Do it yourselves."

Thabiti leaned back. "Really? That's your best idea. We're hardly the Sherlock Holmes and Dr Watsons of Nanyuki. More like Inspector Clouseau and the Pink Panther."

"The Pink Panther wasn't real."

"Neither was Inspector Clouseau," quipped Thabiti, "but that's not the point. How can an old lady and a socially anxious twenty-year-old hope to succeed when the police won't even try?"

Commissioner Akida sat up straight. "You are an intelligent young man, and you have the most to lose or gain."

Thabiti crossed his arms. "OK, I accept that, but Mama Rose... why on earth would she get involved?"

The commissioner leaned forward and said in a low voice, "Few people are aware of what I am about to tell you. A long time ago, your mother was staying with Mama Rose at Ol Kilima Ranch. Poachers entered the homestead and tried to get into the house. Attempting to scare them away, Mama Rose fired a shotgun, but she hit a man and killed him.

"It was a difficult time politically and whilst poaching animals for profit had been made illegal, it was still prolific. Your mother, who was still only a law student, successfully defended Mama Rose before the case reached court. You see, there was a strong bond between them back then and Mama Rose owes your mother much, perhaps even her life."

CHAPTER SEVENTEEN

Rose still felt unsettled. It was Sunday afternoon and Craig appeared content after their Sunday lunch of roast beef fillet, roast potatoes, and carrots and cabbage from their own shamba.

Kipto surprised them with a fruit sponge and custard for pudding, which Craig devoured, but Rose only nibbled. She'd enjoyed the rather strange combination of apples and raspberries, but she worried that the sponge would churn away in her stomach for the rest of the afternoon.

Craig sat on the patio drinking his coffee as he finished his crossword whilst Rose lay along the cedar sofa with Izzy curled up at her feet. Although Nanyuki was peaceful, it was never still. Rose watched a red-striped ladybug fly in circles above her and she heard the buzzing of countless others. Good, she thought. They'll be eating the aphids that are attacking the vegetables in the shamba.

Several dogs barked in sequence as if passing a secret message. All around she could hear the laughter and shouts of children playing and tending to their family's animals. Through this Rose thought she heard the engine of a motorbike, but the noise ceased. She returned to her contemplations.

Suddenly, a ball of white fur, too small to be a sheep, sped around the corner of the patio, and started yapping excitedly at Craig. He looked down and tried to shoo it away by wafting his newspaper, but it continued yapping and spinning in circles.

"There you are," declared a slightly breathless Thabiti, scooping the dog into his arms. His face coloured as he looked up and saw Craig and Rose staring at him in surprise. "Mama Rose, Craig." He almost bowed. "Sorry to interrupt your Sunday afternoon." He darted another look at Craig and turned to flee.

"Thabiti, there's no need to leave. Your dog surprised us, that's all. Would you like coffee? Or there are some cans of Tusker in the fridge in the living room," Craig offered.

"I won't stay long."

"Well, grab me a Tusker and help yourself if you want one," suggested Craig.

"I'm not really a drinker, but a cold Tusker sounds tempting. It's been quite a day."

Thabiti put his dog down and she shot across to Rose's sofa, making energetic but fruitless attempts to jump onto it. Izzy stood up, her fur bristling as she hissed at the dog.

Returning with two cans of beer, Thabiti called, "Pixel" and the little dog ceased her efforts, but remained sitting on her haunches, turning her head to look enquiringly at Thabiti.

"Whose is the dog?" asked Rose, her eyebrows raised.

"Mine, apparently, but I'm not sure what to do. Dr Emma appeared with her this morning, and told me she needed a new home, and that looking after her would comfort me."

The scruffy little dog ran back to Thabiti and tried to climb his legs with its front paws.

Craig indicated to the spare chair. "Take a seat, you're making me nervous. She's certainly taken to you."

"If you want to keep her, I'll help where I can," said Rose.

"I could do with some help, and not just with Pixel. You see Commissioner Akida visited me earlier." Thabiti tugged the ring pull and his beer hissed.

"Did he tell you he was closing the case? He said the same to me this morning." Rose bit her lip.

"I know." Colour flushed in Thabiti's cheeks. "He made out that Ma would understand, that it's the way things are in Kenya. But that's exactly why she did what she did, and fought the system. She never accepted that anything should be brushed aside." Thabiti's entire body racked as tears slid down his face.

"I agree," comforted Rose. "She worked hard, and delved below the surface seeking the truth."

"But there's no one to fight for her, seek out the facts, and bring the culprit to justice."

Rose sighed. Of course, Thabiti was frustrated and upset. "I believe the commissioner knows the decision is wrong, but officially his hands are tied. The only people who really want to establish what happened are us and Pearl."

"I doubt Pearl will help," sniffed Thabiti.

"Then you're on your own," commiserated Rose.

"I'm OK on my own. It's meeting people, talking to them, and asking questions I can't do. I'm useless." He curled forward in his chair, hiding his face while Pixel tried to comfort him.

Rose glanced over at Craig and knew he could read her thoughts. He shook his head. She was not to offer her help.

Craig cleared his throat, "Young man, hard though it is, sometimes we have to let things be. Often it's for the best."

Thabiti looked up, his eyes wide. "You sound like the commissioner." Self-consciously, he hid his head again.

"You owe Ma," Thabiti mumbled. "The commissioner told me what happened."

A cloud moved across the sun, and Rose felt a deep chill. She looked at Craig, but he was staring at his crossword puzzle. How did the commissioner know? How long had he known? Did he see a killer, one who'd escaped justice, every time he looked at her? She realised Thabiti was staring at her, wiping the tears from his face.

"As I said, it's best to let things be. We were younger then, braver," stated Craig.

"Reckless?" questioned Thabiti.

"Perhaps. I realise you want Rose's help, but the commissioner has already asked. She's too old and frail to make enquires in a murder investigation, especially when dangerous people are likely to be involved."

"Old I may be, frail I'm not, nor am I too old to help a friend," Rose bristled. "But none of us has any idea about what's really going on. What your mother was working on, what she found out, or who wanted the investigation stopped."

"But I need to find out. Understand. Move on," pleaded Thabiti.

Craig shrugged helplessly.

"I found this old card on Ma's bedside table and I believe it's your signature inside." Thabiti handed the card to Rose.

She took it, stroking the picture of a guinea fowl on the front. She ached deep inside for the loss of her friend, the fun they'd shared, and the battles they'd fought.

Fighting back her own tears, she said, "She kept this card. Your mother was only twenty-one, a student, like you. She was with me when the trouble happened and she argued my case and won. But our friendship was never the same again. I'm not sure why."

Quietly, Thabiti responded, "Don't you think you owe her, to give her soul peace?"

Rose bit her lip, remembering a young, vibrant Aisha, full of life and colour.

Thabiti reached out his hand, "May I have it back?"

Rose passed him the card.

"Do you remember the line you wrote inside?" When Rose shook her head, he read, "What really matters is invisible to the eyes."

Rose allowed the tears to fall, mourning all that had passed, and as she looked at Craig, he nodded his understanding.

"Yes, Thabiti. I'll help you, whatever trouble it may bring."

CHAPTER EIGHTEEN

On Monday morning, Thabiti rubbed his gluey eyes with the heel of his hand. He opened and quickly closed them against the dazzle of daylight and groaned as the full effects of his hangover hit him: a throbbing head, churning stomach and a kind of vertigo, which was strange since he was still lying down.

Struggling to a sitting position, he swung his legs over the edge of the bed and realised he still wore his jeans. Pixel poked her muzzle out of the disarrayed duvet and, extracting herself, she rubbed against him and yapped. The noise bit through his head.

Stroking her fur, he muttered, "I guess you're hungry?" She barked again in agreement, jumped off the bed, and stood patiently by the closed door. Thabiti heaved himself upright and swayed towards the door, leaning against it to regain his balance, before opening it for Pixel. He lumbered after her.

A chirpy Doris fluttered about the kitchen, singing the words to a Swahili song. She stopped and surveyed Thabiti, with her hands clamped to her bony hips. "I not surprised, you look here." She put her foot on a plastic pedal, opening a small white dustbin. Removing a newspaper, she showed him an array of empty Tusker cans and a small bottle of blended Scottish Whisky.

His stomach lurched, and he stepped quickly away.

"You no drinker, so not start now. This is a sad time, but drink make it worse," she spat. She thrust an envelope into his hand. "Here, you have letter. Wells Fargo man deliver this morning."

Pixel yelped as Doris continued, "I feed dog. You take coffee outside. Fresh air good for you."

Thabiti sat at the cedar table on the veranda, and ignoring his coffee, he drank from a can of coke. He stared at the envelope before him. It was obvious who had sent it from the red embossed crest on the front, with the image of a tree at the centre, and the words "Knowledge is Growth" around the edge. Underneath was stamped "Central University, Nairobi, Kenya". Thabiti hesitated before grabbing the envelope and ripping it open.

He smoothed out the torn letter out and read,

'This letter hereby notifies Thabiti Onyango (the Student) that he is suspended from attendance at Central University, Nairobi for alleged misconduct towards another pupil, Peggy Mwathi. Suspension is not a penalty but a precautionary measure, whilst the necessary investigation takes place. A member of the Investigative Panel may visit the student during this period. The student is prohibited from entering the university during the period of suspension. The student will be notified in writing of the results of the investigation and the action, if any, to be taken against the student.'

Thabiti dropped the letter to the table, pressed his palms to his eyes and leaned back. The letter was not a surprise and, in a way, it was a relief. At last, the university was formally investigating the alleged assault, which was preferable to being judged by his peers on social media. No doubt that would start again.

CHAPTER NINETEEN

Rose was tired, dusty, and thirsty as she turned her trusty red Defender into the rear yard of Guinea Fowl Cottage. Monday mornings were always busy, and today had been no exception.

She'd visited Muguku Farm, fifteen kilometres north of Nanyuki, to check the health and welfare of their dairy and beef herds. Agriculture contributed to over seventy-five per cent of household income in Laikipia County, and employed over forty per cent of the population.

Livestock needed regular checks because of many potentially fatal diseases, such as foot and mouth and various tick-borne sicknesses. Rose's arms were sore from pushing her way through herds of boran cows looking for signs of diarrhoea, nasal discharge, high fevers and depression. One particularly grumpy cow had stamped on her foot, which now throbbed.

Rose parked by the small wooden gate which led to the back of the house and as she climbed out of her Defender, she noticed that the caterer's tent was still in the place. Following the path which led to the front of the house and the guest cottage, she turned into the entrance of the tent.

In her imagination, she expected to find a white outline, such as films used to show the position of a dead body, but the tent was empty apart from five wooden trestle tables. She jumped, her musing disturbed by a slight cough behind her, and she turned to find Doris standing in the entrance.

"Mama Rose, have you come to see her body? The ambulance take her away yesterday."

"Doris, you startled me," admitted Rose. "But I wanted to see the layout of the tent whilst it's still here."

Doris shrugged. "Men be back soon to take the tent and tables. They come this morning and take away crates." She walked over to a table and picked up two pillows and a shuka blanket.

"Did you sleep here on Saturday night?" asked Rose.

"With a dead body? No! But I cover the mistress with the shuka as it chilly night."

"Doris, can you remember precisely where the body was?" Rose searched the ground.

"Here." Doris pointed at a spot in front of a trestle table. Rose screwed up her mouth. "How was she lying?"

Doris lay on the floor. "She like this, Mama. Her eyes scary and open."

"Yes, they were, which is strange. If someone had hit her on the back of the head, she should have been lying face down. Also, you're lying parallel with that table."

"At least she fight," commented Doris.

Rose wrinkled her brow. "How do you know that?"

"Her hand is shut. Make fist. You look for someone with a large bruise. Mistress was strong."

Rose surveyed the tent and asked, "Doris, where is Aisha's head turban?"

The little maid looked blank. As if on cue, a waving length of red and green material entered the tent, held aloft by a grey-haired man wearing blue overalls. "Ladies, you need to clear the tent so we can dismantle it. Does this scarf belong to either of you? We found it in one of our crates."

Rose replied, "I'll take it. Do you have any idea exactly where it was found?" The man looked around at his similarly blue-clad colleague, who shrugged his shoulders. "Never mind. Thank you for returning it." Rose left the tent, turning in the doorway to imprint the layout in her mind.

Doris followed her. "If you want Master Thabiti, he eat lunch outside." In a whisper she said, "He not good. A bad letter come today and I find empty Tusker cans and a bottle of whisky in the rubbish. He try to hide them under Saturday's *Standard* newspaper, but I see these things." She tapped her nose.

CHAPTER TWENTY

Rose left the caterer's tent and continued along the path, past the guest cottage, to the front veranda of Guinea Fowl Cottage. Climbing the steps, she observed a ruffled and unshaven Thabiti sitting at the cedar dining table, hunched over a plate of meat stew into which he dipped a large chunk of bread.

Thabiti spotted her and stopped chewing. "Sorry, I'm not at my best today."

"Had a few drinks last night?" Rose raised her eyebrows.

"Just a few. Well, actually, rather more than that. How did you guess?" Thabiti broke off another piece of bread.

"Oh, the bloodshot eyes, you haven't shaved, and you wore those clothes yesterday. Also, Doris found the empties." She sat down on the wooden bench opposite Thabiti.

"She's like an owl that one. She might appear feather-headed, but she misses nothing." Thabiti dipped the bread in the stew and ate it.

Rose asked, "Were you alone last night or was Pearl here?"

"No, she was out," spluttered Thabiti. "Francis had an important dinner."

Rose leaned forward and touched his arm. "Drinking to numb your grief is understandable. Just as long as you don't make a habit of it."

"I know, I know, but at the moment, well, I just need something and alcohol is the easiest." Thabiti ran his tongue around his lips.

Rose did not press her point, but instead commented, "At least you're eating."

"This stew is delicious. Dr Emma brought it yesterday, when she delivered Pixel." At the sound of her name, the little white dog trotted over from the edge of the veranda. She had been eyeing guinea fowl which were pecking at the front lawn. Thabiti took a sizeable chunk of beef from his plate and dropped it to the floor.

Pixel gulped it down and eyed the top of the table, expecting further plummeting offerings. Thabiti ran another chunk of bread around the rim of his plate to soak up the gravy. He stuffed it into his mouth and chewed vigorously.

"Would you like some?" he asked with his mouth still half-full.

"Do you have anything lighter?" Rose felt her tummy judder.

"Doris," yelled Thabiti. The maid's shrunken but sprightly figure appeared remarkably quickly in the open doorway to the house.

"Yes, Master Thabiti."

Unsurprised, he answered, "Did you say there was fruit salad and yoghurt for pudding? If so, please can you bring a bowl for Mama Rose?"

Doris flitted towards them. "And tea, Mama?"

"You know me well. Yes, please, Doris." Rose sighed gratefully.

When the maid had left, Rose said, "Doris told me you received a letter today which contained distressing news."

Thabiti's shoulders slumped. "How did she know? Yes, a letter arrived from uni. They'd already suggested I didn't return until things settled down as other students had been posting comments on Facebook and WhatsApp."

Thabiti shook his head. "Such spiteful remarks, and just because they don't have to make them to my face. That's one of the reasons we moved here. Even Pearl received cyber abuse."

He pushed his plate away. "I suppose it will begin all over again. The letter was the formal notice of my suspension, until the completion of an investigation into the assault on Peggy Mwathi. The timing's dreadful, but at least the process has begun. But I've no idea how I can prove my innocence."

Rose closed her hand over Thabiti's. "Is there anyone who can help?"

"Not really. My tutor has been in touch and I think he believes that I wasn't involved. I'll speak to him again, sometime, but not today."

Rose lay down the kanga scarf and reached for her glasses and the notebook. "I came to work on a plan for our investigation into your mother's death, but if you would rather not..."

Thabiti sighed. "I did ask you, and I understand the longer an investigation is left, the colder the trail. You lead and I'll try to help where I can."

Rose opened her notebook, smoothed down the first page, and wrote, "Investigation into the Murder of Aisha." Staring at Thabiti, she began, "We need to be clear about Saturday's events. You told the commissioner your mother appeared preoccupied."

Thabiti rubbed his chin. "I've been trying to work that out. At breakfast, she was excited about catching up with old friends. And she'd hosted plenty of parties before, so I don't believe organising another would make her anxious. But if not the party, what else could have disturbed her?"

"Whatever it was, we need to find out. But for the moment, let's stick to what we know and see if we can prepare a timeline. So, the caterers arrived at 4pm?" remembered Rose.

"I believe so. I arrived back just after four and they were unloading their van by the back gate." Rose wrote '4pm' near the top of the page followed by 'caterers arrive'. Below it she wrote 'Thabiti arrives home'.

Thabiti continued, "On the veranda Mum was talking to the large barman."

Rose extracted a crumpled piece of paper from the back of the notebook and consulted it. "Sam," she said, writing the name in her notebook and adding 'talking to Aisha' below her previous entries.

"When I think about it, that was strange. I hadn't realised they were outside until they both raised their voices and started noisily examining cocktail equipment. Mum approached me and handed over her to-do list to check. She also told me to return to town to buy ice. I was away from the house from about half past four until ten past five. It wasn't long after I returned home that you appeared, which I think was about half past five."

Rose nodded. "Yes, an hour early. So the last time you saw your mother was on the veranda between quarter past and half past four."

"Yes." Thabiti rubbed his sore eyes.

"Who else did you see when you first arrived home?" Rose twiddled her pencil.

"The two chefs were in the kitchen unpacking food, with Doris flapping around them. Daniel was carrying items from the van, and Pearl came out of her room and asked for a cup of tea."

"And when you returned a second time with the ice?" asked Rose.

"Much the same. The chefs were in the kitchen, Daniel was sorting cutlery at the dining table, and Sam was on the veranda. After talking with you, I met Pearl who told me she was going to see Ma to borrow a necklace. I asked Doris to take you a cup of tea before I went to my room to shower and change. I was still there when I heard the cry."

Rose frowned, thinking. "Is everyone accounted for?"

"No, I didn't see Francis, but I guess he was in Pearl's room. His car was parked by the garden gate when I first arrived home."

"What sort of car?"

"A Subaru Impreza, a black one, and he knows how to burn rubber with it." Rose spotted a gleam in Thabiti's eyes.

Doris coughed to announce her presence, making them both jump. She placed two bowls on the table containing a jewelled array of pineapple, mango and apple pieces, glistening with the yellow pulp and black seeds of passion fruit.

Rose dolloped a generous spoonful of vanilla yoghurt over hers and licked her spoon in satisfaction. "That's quite a comprehensive account, but it doesn't give us much to go on."

Carefully, Doris set down a china cup of tea by Rose, but a little still splashed into the matching saucer. Rose turned to her and asked, "Did you see anyone in the yard or garden on Saturday, apart from the family and staff? Did anyone visit in the afternoon?"

"No, I see no one," replied Doris, jumping back.

"Did any parcels or letters arrive?" Rose thought something must have sparked the evening's events.

"No. Yes! Mistress Pearl's skirt from the tailor." Doris chewed her thumb.

"And who did you see in the house, after you gave me my tea on Saturday afternoon?"

Doris looked at the sky and back to Rose. "The kitchen is busy. The chefs make small bits of food and put on them on silver trays. They tell Daniel to put them in the tent for later."

"So after you served me tea, Daniel was in and out of the tent?" Rose pressed Doris.

"Yes."

Thabiti looked thoughtful. "There's something about Daniel I just can't place. I thought so the first time I saw him in Dormans, although he avoids eye contact as much as I do."

Rose remembered her last visit to Dormans. "I think he also refused to serve Pearl and Francis last week, but I might have got that wrong."

"Poor boy, have to pay for what that bad man do," Doris spat.

Thabiti and Rose exchanged puzzled looks. "Which poor boy? Do you mean Daniel?" asked Rose.

"Master Thabiti, you play football with Daniel as a small boy. He come to help in the garden, do odd jobs. Nice boy, he carry basket of washing to the drying line for me." Doris tilted her head.

"My brain must be really foggy today, because I've no memory of that." Thabiti shook his head as if to clear it.

"Horrid thing happen after little things go missing," said Doris, wrinkling her nose. "First bits of food, then a sheet and clothes off the washing line. Finally, mistress get very cross. A lovely bronze dish, same shape as the paw of a lion, it vanish. The gardener, Old Moses, he blame Daniel. Everyone believe Moses so Daniel go with no letter and all Nanyuki knows about it. He only get job long way from here.

"But Moses not stop, and try to steal one of the mistress's rings, but I stop him. This time the mistress, she keep quiet and Moses, he 'retire,' but it not help Daniel. Daniel blame your family, and he not forget the shame of it. Oh, no." Doris shook her head dramatically.

"That's tragic," agreed Rose. "And Daniel may have had an opportunity to kill Aisha, but after all this time, is revenge for being sacked a reason to murder her?"

CHAPTER TWENTY-ONE

Rose was visiting Dr Emma's pharmacy when a distraught middle-aged woman rushed in, followed by a blue-overalled African man carrying an open-topped box.

"Please help me." The lady cried. "My dog attacked the tortoise in our garden and its shell is damaged. I'm not sure if there are any other injuries."

Dr Emma signalled for the man to bring the box to the counter. Rose approached the woman, who ran her hands through her shoulder-length dark hair.

"I didn't expect our spaniel to attack the tortoise. She's usually so friendly and playful." The woman's eyes watered.

Rose put her arm around the woman. "Even the best-behaved dogs attack tortoises. I think it's something to do with the tortoise's shape, and the movement of its shell that triggers a reaction. Dogs probably think it's a toy or a football, and try to chew it."

The woman sniffed.

Rose added, "Why don't you go home or for a coffee? We'll call when we've patched up the tortoise." Rose walked the woman out of the door and turned to Dr Emma.

"It's certainly frightened, and hiding under its damaged shell." Dr Emma lifted the tortoise out of the box and examined it. Holding it above her head, she peered at its rear end. "The notch under its tail is U-shaped so we have a mature female weighing around nine kilograms." She handed the frightened reptile to Rose and located a tape measure. "Forty centimetres long."

Dr Emma's pharmacy did not have a separate treatment room, stainless steel operating table or a large overhead light. She cleared a display of dog bowls, cat baskets and a large red hamster cage from a white plastic table and covered it with a frayed towel.

Rose held the tortoise on the table as Dr Emma flushed the puncture wounds and damaged shell with saline solution. The tortoise's head appeared and reared up. Its beak lunged for Rose's hand, but she yanked it away, just in time.

The reptile hissed, a deep primeval sound. Although the tortoise lacked teeth, menacing bony spikes were visible in its gaping mouth. Rose shifted her hands, clutching the sides of the shell firmly.

She heard the clamour of street noise as the shop door opened behind her and Dr Emma looked up and smiled at the customer. "Sorry, we're in the middle of a procedure. Can you pop back in ten minutes?"

There was no response.

Rose concentrated on keeping her patient still.

"You killed him!"

Rose's head shot up. Unable to see the accuser, she watched the startled expression on her colleague's face. The voice was youthful and strong, and it pulsated with anger.

"My dear boy," Dr Emma began in a level tone.

"Don't patronise me. I know what she did." Rose slackened her grip on the shell and the alarmed tortoise attempted to escape. She quickly grabbed it and shivered.

"We're vets. We try to save animals, but sometimes we're unsuccessful. I am sorry for your loss. Was it your dog?" asked Dr Emma.

"Dog! What are you talking about? She shot my grandfather."

"Don't be ridiculous. Why on earth would Rose do that?"

Slowly, Rose loosened her grip on the tortoise and turned to face her accuser. She said, "He doesn't mean now, do you? You mean long ago, before you were born?"

"Yes, my dad was only a baby. He never knew his father."

"So why come looking for me now?" Rose asked.

"I seek justice. Someone has to pay." The young man pointed his finger at her.

"What justice can I give you? It's been forty years, and I'm an old lady now." Rose held out her hands in a conciliatory gesture.

"Justice. What rot. Money's what he's after. You heard him say someone has to pay." Dr Emma clenched her jaw.

"She can't protect you now, and I'm not afraid of her sidekick, despite his size." The young man puffed out his chest.

Rose felt numb, but her mind raced. Who was he talking about? Was "she" Aisha? Aisha had inferred that the case hadn't been officially reopened, and that she'd just begun sifting through old files. She hadn't mentioned returning to Ol Kilima to ask questions. And if it was Aisha, who was her sidekick?

Dr Emma surged forward and glared up at the man. "Enough of this. Get out." He stood his ground. The diminutive Dr Emma was a comical sight as she bravely shooed the man away, wearing her blue surgical gloves and gown.

"I'm not going anywhere. I want what I came for." The young man leaned forward, his teeth bared.

Dr Emma recoiled, regained her composure, and appeared to rise in stature. "Out. I won't have drunken men in MY pharmacy, slinging accusations at MY colleague."

The man finally turned to leave the shop. He stopped and looked back, meeting Rose's eyes. "I know who you are now, and I'm not finished. You owe my family, and you'll pay for what you did."

"Get out!" screamed Dr Emma. She slammed the door and slumped against it, facing Rose. Glancing at the table, she rushed forward. Rose remembered the tortoise, which was balancing precariously on the edge of the table. It extended its neck to peer at the floor and toppled over.

Rose caught it, but the weight carried her to the floor like a ship's anchor. She sat up. "Ow! It bit me."

Dr Emma took the tortoise and helped Rose to her feet. "That man was angry and drunk, a bad combination." The tortoise hissed. "But you knew what he was talking about, didn't you? I can't believe you'd deliberately hurt anyone. If you need my help, just ask. Now let's finish this. Tip her onto her side."

Dr Emma took a beaker of sugar and poured it into one of the tortoise's puncture wounds. She placed a piece of soft gauze over the wound and secured it in place with cotton tape.

Rose's voice was distant. "Yes, I know what he was worked up about. I thought the matter was buried, and the trauma healed by time, but now it's out in the open, and festering away in that young man's mind."

Rose's focus returned to the present as she manoeuvred the tortoise so Dr Emma could treat the other wounds.

"Sugar, a natural remedy. It's far better to let nature take its course. The sugar absorbs moisture, no moisture means no bacteria and so the wound can begin to heal."

The treatment complete, Dr Emma stepped back, and revealed, "I'm shaking. It must have been the encounter with that angry young man. She peeled off her gloves and reached below the cash desk, extracting a dusty bottle of brandy. "If you put the tortoise back in its box, I'll rinse some mugs. I think we both need a drop of this," she said, waving the bottle. "Purely medicinal, of course."

CHAPTER TWENTY-TWO

Later on Monday afternoon, Rose stretched out along the large wooden sofa on her covered patio. Her eyes were closed and she felt weak and light-headed, which might be due to the generous measure of brandy Dr Emma had poured.

A week ago, her greatest worry was whether there would be sufficient funds, and time, to run all the rabies vaccination clinics needed in the Nanyuki area.

She always had financial worries, but she'd got used to them. As long as there was enough food for her animals and Craig, and sufficient money to pay the staff, rent and bills at the end of the month, she was content. She didn't crave smart clothes, expensive jewellery or foreign holidays, at least not ones "in the sun".

The young man at the pharmacy troubled her. In the end, she felt it would come down to money. Compensation to the family for shooting his grandfather. It was likely, even inevitable, that they had suffered in poverty when the man of the house was killed. Like so many Kenyans, she knew what it was like to go hungry.

But the young man's anger really worried her as it could lead to violence against her, her friends and family, or even innocent people, especially if fuelled by alcohol. But it was violence, her violence, which had landed them in this predicament.

"Rose, are you OK?" Craig asked, his brow wrinkled.

"I'm not sure." Rose looked at Craig as she hugged her knees to her chest. "An indignant young man found me in Dr Emma's pharmacy. He claimed to be the grandson of the man I shot at Ol Kilima, and he wanted payment for what I'd done."

"The grandson. Where has he suddenly appeared from and why now?"

Rose kept silent.

"Was he after money?" Craig pressed.

"That was Dr Emma's conclusion. And according to her, he was drunk, so it's difficult to determine what he really wanted." Rose rocked back and forth, still hugging her knees.

"I am sorry this is being dragged up all over again. And that I wasn't at Ol Kilima to help you that day, but I can support you now. If he accosts you again in town, move somewhere public. If he wants a showdown or gets angry, walk away or get help. You have many friends in Nanyuki, as you've helped lots of people. If he wants to talk further, I'll meet him. But there's not much we can do now except wait, so let's have a crack at this crossword I've just printed."

Rose uncurled her legs. "You'll have to read it, as I've no idea where my glasses are."

Craig read, "One down, five letters, 'an evil being which may be cast out'."

Rose's phone pinged.

"That'll be a text message. Do you want me to read it?" Craig asked.

"Please. I hope it's not a request to stitch a cow, but when duty calls…"

"It's from Thabiti. He's found your glasses and notebook, and he might have a development in the case."

She sat up and announced, "Some good news at last. I'll drive over there now, as I can't really concentrate on your crossword at the moment. But tell me, what's the answer to that clue?"

"Demon."

"How apt. Are you coming?"

"If you don't mind, I'll stay here. You can tell me all about it over supper. What delight does Kipto have for us today?"

"Mince, in some form, which I bought from Jack Wright Butchers." Rose paused, summoning her strength. She watched a pair of small red-cheeked cordon-bleu finches peck at the stone bird table before departing to find other delights. She kissed Craig on the cheek and left.

CHAPTER TWENTY-THREE

It was early Monday evening when Rose returned to Guinea Fowl Cottage and found Pearl sitting at the dining table on the veranda, sketching on a pad of plain paper. Rose noted an eclectic mix of household items strewn across the tabletop.

"Good evening, Pearl. How are you?"

Pearl looked up, twisting her earring. "It's rather like being in a dream, but the other way around. I know this is reality, but it feels like an illusion. I rather like it, as it's mystical and peaceful. And nobody's telling me what to do."

"I'm glad to see you're taking your mind off things."

Pearl brightened and swivelled her sketchpad round to face Rose. "Do you like them? I'm designing skirts. I do love the bright colours of kanga. Ladies traditionally just wrap the rectangles of cloth around themselves, or have a simple skirt made. But wouldn't it be great to explore more elaborate designs?" Pearl sucked the end of her pencil.

"What a lovely idea," said Rose, delighted to see Pearl applying herself to such a task.

Rose glanced around. "Is Thabiti about? He sent me a text."

"He was very excited about our discovery of a bag of goodies hidden in a flower bed. But when he saw it was just some bits and pieces from the house, he slouched inside."

"Ah, there you are, Pearl." Francis strode onto the veranda, resplendent in a grey suit and a fat knot of red tie. "I'm a little late."

He looked at Pearl, and his face tightened. "Can't you even get yourself dressed? Hurry up and get changed." Pearl stood and drifted towards the house. "Come on, I'll help you." Francis placed his hand on her back and propelled her through the open door.

Rose tidied Pearl's sketchpad and pencils and retrieved her notebook and glasses, which she spotted amongst the many items on the table. She examined a bottle of expensive shampoo, a small box of Amoxil tablets, and then held aloft a set of car keys.

"The spare keys to Ma's Prado," Thabiti remarked, coming to stand beside her with a bottle of Tusker beer in his hand. "All these items were found by a casual gardener this afternoon, in an old blue bag, hidden in a flower bed by the side door."

"It's a rather strange selection. Any idea who put it there, or where they got everything from?"

Thabiti separated pill boxes, shampoos, lotions and perfume bottles. "These, I believe, were taken from the main bathroom which Pearl uses and the food items from the kitchen or dhobi room cupboards. The car keys were hanging on a key rack by the back door, and Pearl's trainers, well, they could have been lying around anywhere."

Rose considered the collection and said, "It looks to me like an opportunistic thief, grabbing whatever he or she could find at hand. Had you noticed any of these items were missing?"

"No, not with everything else that's going on." Thabiti took a long swig his beer.

"I understood last night was a one-off, that you rarely drank."

"I don't. It's just one beer and I need it. It's been a difficult day."

Rose wrinkled her brow, but decided not to pursue the discussion.

Thabiti shifted through the items. "Would someone kill over these, do you think? They don't look hugely valuable."

"They're probably worth a few months' wages," replied Rose. "Significantly more if you count the Prado. If this thief has a respectable job which allows him access to houses he can plunder, then you're looking at someone who regularly supplements his income. The stakes become much higher, possibly worth killing for."

"Any suggestions?" asked Thabiti.

Rose leant against the table and responded, "One of the catering crew, or the barman, Sam. I'm sure there were a number of times he could have moved around the house unobserved."

"I think this is Daniel settling a score with us," announced Thabiti.

"What, by doing the very deed he was accused of?"

Thabiti's eyebrows drew together. "Why not? But would he kill over it?"

Francis coughed behind them and they both started. How long had he been standing there and what had he overheard?

Francis leaned over the table. "Pearl told me you'd found a bag of loot. Not very impressive, is it?" He wrinkled his nose. "I saw the waiter, Daniel, with that bag. He's a slippery character, that one, and I wouldn't trust him as far as I could throw him."

Francis stood up and addressed Thabiti. "I hope it's OK, but Pearl will be staying with me tonight. We're attending a dinner in Meru and it'll finish too late to drive back here." He nodded, and said politely, "Goodnight."

Rose watched Francis leave, and then turned to Thabiti and suggested, "We should meet tomorrow for coffee."

Thabiti shrugged. "Sure, come round. I expect I shall be in all morning."

"No, not here." She placed a hand on Thabiti's arm. "At Dormans, so we can catch up with a certain waiter."

Thabiti looked panic stricken and started to blow out short breaths as he gradually gained control. "I don't think I can do that. Not with all those people knowing what happened. And they'll be looking at me, judging me and talking about me."

Rose squeezed his arm. "True, this is Nanyuki, and the death of your mother will be the main news item. But don't worry, I'll be there. You'll have to face people sooner or later."

"I'd prefer later."

"Well, if you want to make it harder for people to recognise you, come in disguise."

"What as?" Thabiti narrowed his eyes.

"Not a costume." Rose raised her hands. "Just wear a basketball cap, dark glasses and a hood."

Thabiti smiled, "I think you mean a baseball cap and a hoody. A hood is a gangster, and whilst bringing one would deflect attention from me, there's no way Daniel would talk to us."

"Don't get smart with me. I'm only trying to help." There was a small yap from under the table and Pixel emerged.

"Sit," said Thabiti, but the dog stood, wagging her tail.

"Not like that. You need to use a firmer tone," remonstrated Rose.

She stood opposite Pixel, and using a clear voice commanded, "SIT!" At the same time, she held her hand above the dog's head, palm down, and gestured towards the floor. Pixel looked at her warily, but nonetheless obeyed her. "Good girl. Now your turn, Thabiti."

He started waving his hand about, but eventually he combined the correct hand gesture with a firm "SIT!" and Pixel did.

Rose patted his shoulder. "See, it's not so difficult. So shall we meet tomorrow at eleven, after my morning appointments?"

"I really don't think I can." Thabiti shook his head.

"Thabiti!" Rose said in a firmer tone, as if speaking to Pixel again.

"OK, OK," he conceded.

Rose opened the first page of her notebook, which was empty apart from her initial jottings. "I think you'd better record our findings, as I get too caught up in the moment to write anything down."

"No problem." Thabiti removed his phone from his pocket and photographed the items strewn across the table. "Done."

"Done what? You didn't write anything."

"I don't need to. I store information on my phone as pictures and voice files, as well as written notes. Neat, isn't it?"

"Beyond me," responded Rose.

CHAPTER TWENTY-FOUR

Dormans coffee shop was quiet and dusty on Tuesday morning. The enticing smells of baking croissants, pastries and muffins wafted through the air.

Rose had completed her morning's work injecting a string of polo ponies with rabies vaccinations. She was concerned about three of them, whose coats were rough and dull, rather than shiny like their companions'.

She needed to put together her digestive herbal mix. It could be added to their daily feeds to improve the ability of their digestive tracts to break down food and release more vitamins and nutrients. Their owner wanted them fit and healthy for the imminent start of the polo season.

Several street sellers called out to her before she walked into Dormans' courtyard, and she exchanged greetings with them. Thabiti was not there. She hoped he wouldn't let her down. She spotted Chloe, the attractive blonde-haired lady who was new to Nanyuki.

"Cooee," Chloe called as she stood up behind the same table they had occupied when Rose had first met her for coffee.

Rose walked across to her table.

"It's lovely to see you again, and I owe you coffee. It was so rude of me to leave you to pay the bill last time, when you clearly had so little money," Chloe blurted. "Please join me. I feel like a flower on one of these plants, colourful and admired but, after a glance, ignored." She bit her bottom lip.

Rose hesitated. How could she refuse Chloe's request without appearing rude? Chloe tugged on her arm. She relented and sat down. At least she could see the entrance from her vantage point on the wooden picnic bench and she hoped Thabiti turned up soon, as she wasn't sure how to interview Daniel on her own.

She'd agreed to help Thabiti investigate his mother's death, but she had a nagging feeling about his commitment, particularly when public places were involved. Turning back, she realised Chloe was chattering away to her.

"You know you were right about the coffee. Too much makes me very woozy so I've switched to freshly squeezed fruit juices and smoothies… without the added sugar."

Chloe pointed proudly to a tall glass brimming with a thick magenta liquid. She put a straw to her lips and sucked enthusiastically. She let go of the straw, grimacing and turning the same colour as her drink. Finally she managed to splutter, "Oh, that's sharp!"

Rose tried to control her laughter, but failed. "I admire your spirit for trying something new, but tree tomato juice is really astringent. You have to add some sugar syrup."

Looking over at the entrance again, Rose thought she spotted Thabiti. A man had arrived wearing a scarlet beanie hat pulled low over his eyebrows, and large, dark sunglasses. He was hunched and looked furtively around the coffee shop. Eyeing Rose, he scuttled sideways, crablike, to her table and slid onto the seat next to her. It was hardly an unobtrusive entrance.

Rose eyed him closely. His beard and moustache were neat, and he wore a clean navy polo shirt, but his constant mouth movements betrayed the gum he chewed. He lifted his dark glasses and rubbed at his eyes, which had a pink sheen.

"Another tough night?" she remarked.

"Yes," he answered morosely, folding his arms on top of the table and resting his head on them.

Rose was about to lecture him, but swallowed and decided to leave it for now. He had enough to contend with.

Chloe interrupted her thoughts with a bright introduction to Thabiti. "Hi, I'm Chloe!"

He looked up, focused properly on Chloe, and quickly replaced his dark glasses. "Hi, Thabiti." He looked down at the table.

In an apologetic tone, Rose explained, "Thabiti struggles to meet new people, particularly after a challenging few days."

"Tell me about it," exclaimed Chloe, launching into a list of her own woes. "The electricity cuts out every night, and the back-up generator refuses to kick in, so I have to call the guard to start it by hand. There's no hot water in the kitchen, and every time I try to have a shower I get electrocuted."

When she stopped to take a breath, Rose interrupted her and said, "That's all very annoying, but I'm afraid they're typical problems of living in a Kenyan house." As Thabiti reached over to the adjacent table for a napkin, into which he spat his gum, Rose whispered, "His mother died on Saturday."

Chloe's hand shot to her mouth as she squawked. She leaned towards Thabiti and patted his arm. "I'm so sorry for your loss."

He shrank back from her touch, but responded automatically. "Oh, thank you."

"Was she ill a long time?"

"Oh no, she wasn't ill."

"So, an accident?"

"The police are calling it that, despite telling me she was struck on the head."

CHAPTER TWENTY-FIVE

"MURDER," Chloe mouthed in an exaggerated stage whisper. She was sitting with Rose and Thabiti on the courtyard of Dormans coffee shop.

Chloe's shining eyes betrayed her excitement. "What are we going to do?"

"There's nothing you can do." Thabiti lowered his head to the tabletop.

"Actually," announced Rose, "you need some sugar syrup for your tree tomato juice, and we need to order our drinks. Could you ask the waiter over there to come and serve us?"

Chloe's shoulders drooped in disappointment. "Oh, OK. The waiter who served us last time?"

"Yes, Daniel." Rose's voice sounded even to her ears, but her insides were fluttering. This was real. She had to interview a suspect. Someone who could be dangerous. He might have killed Aisha.

Chloe rose, straightened non-existent creases from her red tailored shorts, and strode expertly, in her matching high heels, to a far table which Daniel was clearing. She towered over him and Rose realised how elflike he was with small pointy ears and a neat little pointed beard. But his movements were stealthy rather than sprightly.

He approached their table and recognised Thabiti, still prostrate on the table, and a look of malice entered his eyes. Chloe was quick to grab his sleeve as he turned to leave.

Rose took a deep breath to steady herself and began, "Hi, Daniel. Please sit down and join us for a few minutes." Was she being too formal? Should she be more abrupt and assertive?

Daniel remained standing and glared at her. "I've nothing to say in his presence. And why should I talk to you? You're not the police."

"Well, put it this way," Rose replied, "I'm going to ask you some questions about Saturday night, even if I have to shout them across the forecourt." Thabiti looked at her wide-eyed, but she ignored him.

"That might be rather embarrassing, so I suggest you just sit down." Rose used the same tone she had with Pixel the day before, and Daniel complied. She was in her stride now. She wasn't going to let this young man get the better of her.

Daniel slumped onto the vacant wooden seat next to Chloe. Ignoring Thabiti, and staring definitely at Rose, he asked, "What am I accused of this time?"

"I'm not accusing you of anything. I just need to clear up some loose ends. Did you notice anyone on Saturday evening with an old blue bag?"

"Yes me. Did you find it? Was my grey fleece inside?"

Rose looked over at Thabiti. "Have you seen a grey fleece?"

He shook his head.

"I'll ask Doris to look for it. Now there's no need to screw your face up like that. She has nothing but kind words to say about you."

Daniel opened his hands on the table. "She was good to me, and often shared her ugali and bean lunch. So why are you interested in my old bag?"

"Because someone filled it with stolen items from Guinea Fowl Cottage. A gardener found it hidden in a flower bed yesterday."

Rose felt Daniel bristle as he sat back and crossed his arms. She realised she was losing him so continued quickly, "I'm not saying it was you, but did you see anyone, in particular one of your colleagues, creeping around the house or in rooms they shouldn't have been in?"

Daniel gave her a sly look. "What's in it for me?" Oh dear, thought Rose, this isn't going very well. She wished Thabiti would help her.

"Do you only do something for payment?" asked Chloe. It was an interesting question, and Rose wondered where she was going with it.

"What's it to you?"

Chloe squared her shoulders and replied, "There's no need to be rude, but I noticed you're wearing a TAG watch."

"So he is." Agreed Thabiti sitting up. "Where did you get that from? And more to the point, how did you PAY for it?"

Daniel covered his left wrist and mumbled, "It's a fake."

"No, it's not." Swiftly and deftly, Chloe pulled his right hand away and tilted the watch. "The face has a violet tint from the sapphire coating."

Daniel snatched both hands away and leapt up from the table. "I didn't see anyone, and I didn't steal anything." He slipped away.

"He didn't even take our order," Thabiti mused. "Luckily, I'm not thirsty."

CHAPTER TWENTY-SIX

At a corner table outside Dormans coffee shop, Rose turned to Thabiti and said, "I think that's two out of ten for my interview technique. I failed to find out anything new and you weren't much help."

"It's puzzling, though," mused Chloe. "From what you've told me about the meagre Kenyan wages, I can't work out how Daniel could afford a TAG watch, or the shoes and belt he was wearing. They're expensive items."

Rose perked up. Maybe her talk with Daniel hadn't been a complete disaster. "I've no idea about their value, but I think you're on to something. Maybe someone paid him off, but what for?"

"Oh, it's like being in a movie! Perhaps someone hired Daniel to commit the murder," exclaimed Chloe.

"Please! This is my Ma," groaned Thabiti.

"But she has a point. We've no idea who Daniel was involved with when he was away from Nanyuki. And it's conceivable he could have been paid to commit the crime, especially since he still bears a grudge against your family."

Her eyes gleaming with excitement, Chloe declared, "So, we have a motive, a grudge you say, and payment for a hit from some mobster. What about the means and opportunity?"

"Chloe, please, don't be so dramatic," pleaded Thabiti. "Someone from Nairobi could have paid him, but it's more likely to be some corrupt government official than a gangster."

"Opportunity," mused Rose. "Doris told me Daniel was in and out of the house and tent all afternoon. But what about means? And we haven't considered the murder weapon."

"I'm not aware of anything being found on our compound," replied Thabiti.

"What was in the tent?" asked Rose. She drummed her fingers on the table.

Thabiti bit his bottom lip. "I saw Daniel carrying red crates with crockery, cutlery and platters. But I doubt any of them could have been used as a weapon."

"Death by teaspoon," Chloe cried, but noticing Thabiti's pained expression, she added, "What about a rolling pin?"

"Yes, that's a possibility," agreed Thabiti. "Doris will have at least one in the house, even if the caterers didn't bring their own. I'll ask her if one's missing."

Rose was thoughtful. "A rolling pin is an excellent suggestion, or a wooden board whose edge could have been swung at her. Oh, I'm sorry, Thabiti," she turned and held his arm, "This is all rather morbid, but please bear with me. The commissioner gave the impression that a precise blow was delivered to the base of the skull. So the implement we seek is not sharp, nor is it too large or heavy."

Thabiti winced. He jumped to his feet and raced inside the coffee shop. Rose suspected he would run straight out the back and down the metal stairs to the loos. He had turned a pallid shade during her last statement.

"Do you think he left to throw up?" asked Chloe. "It is one of the best cures for a hangover."

CHAPTER TWENTY-SEVEN

Late on Tuesday afternoon, Rose sat on the cedar sofa on her covered patio, slowly tapping the screen of her iPad. She completed the email to her daughter, Heather, with 'Love Mum' and clicked the 'Send' symbol.

She found typing on the small screen sore with her misshapen fingers, the knuckles of which had permanently swollen to form firm nodules. Heather had presented her with the iPad on her last visit to Kenya, as she wrongly presumed Rose's intermittent emails were down to a dislike for typing, rather than the distraction of other events and activities.

Once Rose found the time, she enjoyed writing to Heather. Her daughter might live in the UK, married and with her own daughters, but she'd grown up in the county of Laikipia, of which Nanyuki was the administrative capital.

Rose hoped her stories about the happenings and characters of the area entertained her daughter. She knew Heather and her brother, Chris's, childhood had been hard as the family learnt to exist on very little, but she hoped it had been a happy one.

She put down the iPad and looked across at Craig. "You needn't nag me this week. I've emailed Heather and filled her in on the murder. It's rather a different topic from the usual problematic cow pregnancies or abscesses on sheep."

"Did you enquire if she's booked her flights for the summer and whether it's just her or the entire family?" asked Craig.

"I didn't. You'll have to ask her. And anyway, I don't like to nag. They're so busy with their own lives."

Craig's shoulders slumped. "But we're not getting any younger and… "

Rose's phone rang, interrupting him.

"Hello? Rose speaking."

"Habari, Mama Rose." Commissioner Akida greeted her. "I would like to meet up with you and Thabiti at Guinea Fowl Cottage. Will you be free at six o'clock tonight?"

Rose glanced at her watch. "In half an hour. Yes, I'll see you there."

When she finished the call, Craig asked, "Do I have to eat supper alone again?" He crossed his arms.

"Why don't you come with me? I'm sure the commissioner will be glad to see you."

"I don't want to be a hindrance." Rose recognised his tone. Craig had always respected her independence, even relied on it at times, but lately he had become a little tetchy, which was probably the result of his own increasing health issues. But languishing at home only made him worse.

Rose proclaimed, "It will do you good to get out."

CHAPTER TWENTY-EIGHT

Thabiti sat at the cedar dining table on Tuesday afternoon with both his and his mother's laptops open in front of him.

"Do I have to wear this dress again? You promised to buy me the blue, ankle-length one in Daphne's window."

Thabiti clicked his tongue in annoyance. Pearl's plea had broken his concentration, and just when he thought he understood the security software on Ma's laptop, which was surprisingly cutting edge. He sighed. The heat had been relentless today, even under the shade of the veranda.

He flipped the top off a bottle of Tangawizi Ginger Beer and savoured the burning sensation inside his nose from its powerful ginger aroma. Further words carried through the open windows from the house.

"I'm a bit short at the moment," responded Francis. "Just a temporary cash flow issue, which I'm dealing with. I expect to be back in funds by the end of the week, and then I can buy that dress you so admire. But what about you, my dear? You'll be getting your own money soon. And plenty of it, I expect."

Thabiti frowned and leaned towards the window. Where was this conversation heading?

"Oh, will I? It would be nice to buy, or do things, without always begging for money."

"What provision does your mother's will set out?"

Thabiti sat up. He hadn't considered a will, and Ma had never mentioned one. Would she have held it herself, or entrusted it to another lawyer? No, she wouldn't have trusted anyone else, so she must have kept it. He'd better start looking.

He heard Francis say, "When you come into your inheritance, I know of a nice little scheme, which involves water. Simple, but vital. It's important you invest your money wisely so it can grow. Now, I'll let you get changed."

Thabiti's stomach tightened. He didn't like the sound of Francis's scheme. He returned to the laptop, but a shadow fell across his keyboard.

"May I join you?" Francis scissored his legs over the bench, placing a cut-glass tumbler of amber liquid before him. Thabiti sat back, gripping the table. Francis's affability unsettled him and he wanted a drink, the sweet smell of the brandy igniting his desire for alcohol.

Francis began, "My mother died when I was a boy. At least you have Pearl. I also lost my sister, and she was just ten years old."

Thabiti dropped his hands, unnerved by this revelation and the apparent act of sympathy. Francis appeared upset as he took a gulp of brandy and stared into the distance. Thabiti wondered how to respond as the usual, arrogant Francis he'd learned to ignore.

"I'm worried about Pearl. She seems to live in her own world, and fantasises about things she thinks she's seen, heard or done." Francis swirled his drink. "It's all very worrying."

Thabiti screwed up his eyes but didn't respond.

Francis drained his glass, pushed the bench back, and stood up.

Thabit winced as Francis patted him on the shoulder and announced, "I can see you're busy so I won't disturb you further."

CHAPTER TWENTY-NINE

Rose and Craig pulled up at the rear of Guinea Fowl Cottage as Commissioner Akida arrived in his official blue Land Cruiser pickup. It was a heavy vehicle, utilitarian, with benches in the back for transporting officers and prisoners and a canvas cover to protect them from harsh sunshine or heavy downpours.

The commissioner walked across to assist Craig as he manoeuvred himself out of Rose's Defender. Once on his feet, but leaning against the vehicle, Craig said, "Thank you. Much appreciated, Commissioner."

They walked steadily to the front of the house, with the commissioner assisting Craig by allowing him to lean on his arm. As they climbed the veranda steps together, Rose saw Thabiti sitting at the far end of the dining table with two open laptops.

She realised the man talking to him, almost conspiratorially, was Francis. He turned and when he saw them, he drained the golden contents of his tumbler and rose from the table. He patted Thabiti on the shoulder before striding into the house without acknowledging Rose or her companions.

Frowning, Rose thought it out of character of Francis to need a stiff drink, especially so early in the evening. He always seemed so confident and in complete control of himself. Thabiti also stood up, closed the laptops, and shuffled over to meet them, blinking rapidly.

He stood and greeted them apologetically. "Hi, forgive me. I'm feeling a little anxious." He gulped. "Let's sit on the wicker chairs."

The commissioner jumped back. "That cushion moved!" They followed his gaze as Pixel uncurled herself, looking up with large, beseeching eyes.

Grinning, his nervousness retreating, Thabiti asked, "Would you like a drink?"

He left to find Tuskers for himself and Craig, and a Whitecap for the commissioner.

Rose had asked for a small glass of white wine. As she made herself comfortable on the sofa, Pixel sat up, rearranged herself and placed her head in Rose's lap, once more feigning sleep.

Thabiti returned with the drinks and sat down next to Rose, stroking Pixel's back. Had Pixel been a cat, Rose was certain she would have purred loudly in contentment.

Rose turned to Thabiti and remarked, "I'm pleased to see you and Francis are getting on. I wasn't sure how you felt about him and his relationship with your sister."

"To be honest, I'm still not sure, particularly after part of a conversation I just overheard."

"Why? What was it about?"

"Money. Pearl didn't want to wear a particular dress to a party tonight, but Francis said she had to as he hadn't bought her another one. He said he was short of money until the end of the week."

"But payday isn't until the end of the month. I wonder where those funds are coming from," mused Rose, almost to herself.

"I was surprised when he came and sat with me, and told me about losing his mother and sister when he was a boy."

"His sister was only ten, if I remember correctly," pronounced the commissioner. "They both contracted an infection and died. It happened very quickly, but Francis's father was devastated. I had forgotten about the son until we met Francis on Saturday evening. I must say, he's done very well for himself."

CHAPTER THIRTY

On Tuesday evening, Rose sat on the veranda of Guinea Fowl Cottage with Craig, Thabiti and Commissioner Akida.

The commissioner cleared his throat and began, "Thank you for meeting me this evening. I wanted to review the information you have gathered." He removed his penknife from one pocket and a small piece of wood from another, and absent-mindedly began whittling.

Rose summarised the bag of stolen items they'd found, their interview with Daniel, their observations about his newfound wealth, his unwillingness to tell them all he knew, and his history with the Onyango family.

"You are certain Daniel is caught up in this business, but you don't have the bait to hook him. So you need to discover the role he played, and whether it was robbery, murder… or something else. It is all very fishy. Can I suggest you interview the rest of the catering staff again."

"Quite so, Commissioner," said Craig. "But Rose and Thabiti need to find the right opportunity to do that."

The commissioner put down his knife and the small carving he had begun. He patted his pockets and extracted a white envelope from inside his jacket. It was addressed using his full title and contained a thick embossed invitation on which was written, in gold italics, *Grand Opening of the Crown Casino, Nanyuki.*

The commissioner tapped the invitation and remarked, "If you look towards the bottom, you will note that Avocado Catering is providing refreshments, so that is where our chefs will be tomorrow. I am not sure about the barman as the casino will provide their own drinks."

"But Rose and Thabiti can't just walk in and start questioning them. They don't have invitations, for a start," responded Craig.

"And there will be way too many people." Thabiti shuddered.

The commissioner sat back. "The chefs will begin preparing food before the event starts, so just devise a plan to gain early access."

"Oh, I could wear a disguise," beamed Thabiti.

"Oh Thabiti, have you been invited to the opening party for the casino tomorrow night as well?" Pearl asked, her eyes widening. "We're going, aren't we, darling?" She addressed Francis, who had walked with her from the house, but was hanging back, unwilling to join the group.

Pearl looked glamorous in a gold silk dress, which had long slits up each side, accentuating her slim legs. Francis was smartly turned out in his shimmering black dinner suit, with a gold bow tie to match Pearl's dress. But he appeared preoccupied, and Rose noticed a nick on his chin, where he had cut himself shaving.

"Darling!" Pearl said a little louder.

Francis finally focused on the conversation. "Oh, yes, the opening of the casino. We shall be in the VIP lounge… far more profitable."

"Because you'll be able to gamble more? Are the stakes higher?" asked Rose.

"Oh no. I don't play games of chance, but I will have the opportunity to win over several important business people and politicians. They're visiting from many of the major cities, including Nairobi, Mombasa and Eldoret. Consider how rewarding it would be to build casinos in all those areas."

"You look bonnie, Pearl," said Rose. "Where are you heading tonight?"

His condescension returning, Francis answered, "We are attending a dinner as the personal guests of Mr Jeremiah Angote."

"Oh, who's he?" asked Rose. "He sounds important."

The commissioner answered. "He provides medical and healthcare equipment to many of the county governments." He considered Francis intently.

"That's right, Commissioner. And we need new X-ray equipment for Timau Ward."

The commissioner's eyes narrowed. "Is that your own Ward?"

"Yes. I grew up in Timau." Francis brushed the sleeve of his jacket.

"I knew your father. A hard-working and self-reliant man, but I have not seen him since... the tragedy." The commissioner held Francis's gaze.

Tight-lipped, Francis responded, "He still has the shop. And I visit him occasionally, but he is a sad old man, blaming himself for what happened."

Pearl interrupted, "I think we should leave. We don't want to be late for the champagne reception."

After they left, Rose asked, "I wonder why Francis was brooding?"

"I am not sure I approve of his fraternising with Jeremiah Angote."

"Why, Commissioner?" asked Craig.

"He is becoming a rich and powerful man, and according to an article written in last Saturday's

Standard, not by entirely legal methods. The inference being he has given financial kickbacks to local government officials in return for being awarded government contracts. It's believed he's now supplying equipment and healthcare products to over sixty percent of county governments."

A distraught Doris ran up the veranda steps. "Master Thabiti, the cottage, break-in, things missing."

"What things?" asked the commissioner sharply.

"Mistress's computer, papers, files. They clever, no mess, but I knows someone there, look about."

Thabiti let out a lengthy breath. "I took the laptop and I may have moved some papers on her desk. It must have been me."

"The computer is safe." Doris pressed her hand to her heart. "But I knows someone else in cottage. Come, come." She gestured to Thabiti with her hand and ran back down the veranda steps.

With a sigh, Thabiti followed Doris to the guest cottage in the garden.

Rose stood at the open front door with the commissioner and thought nothing looked amiss.

There were no dislodged books, upturned furniture or objects strewn across the floor. It all looked neat and tidy. She asked, "Did your mother spend much time in this cottage?"

"Yes," replied Thabiti. "And she'd taken to sleeping here as well." He stood with Doris beside the desk. "When I collected Ma's laptop yesterday, it was here, on the desk, and so were these papers." He bit his bottom lip. "And behind it were stacked several files, but they're not here anymore."

"And bottom drawer empty, look, and mistress always lock it," added Doris.

"I wonder what was special about those particular files?" Thabiti mused.

Rose's forehead prickled. Was the grey box file Aisha had showed her missing? The one about the incident at Ol Kilima? And were the others also linked to poaching and the shooting? What if the poacher's grandson had taken them?

Rose breathed in deeply and slowly exhaled. How would he know about the files and, if he did, how would he know where to look for them?

Rose didn't think the grandson was the burglar. He seemed hot-headed and more likely to act on the-spur-of-the-moment, and if he had broken in he would definitely have searched for valuables and left a mess. No, this was someone who knew exactly what they wanted, and they'd been very methodical in their search. But what if they returned for Aisha's laptop?

The commissioner called to Doris. "When were you last in here?"

"I sort the mistress's clothes on Monday. Most I pack in cardboard boxes for Mama Rose, for her charities. I take few things for me, Master Thabiti said OK." Doris pouted.

Rose smiled at Doris. "I'm sure Aisha would want you to have some of her clothes. And it's kind of you to think of less the fortunate women I support. Remind me to take those boxes when I leave."

"It Master Thabiti's idea. He said you help ladies with bad husbands, and they happy to get the mistress's clothes."

Rose looked at Thabiti, who did not meet her eyes. Instead he said, "I was in here yesterday morning collecting Ma's laptop, which I was working on before you arrived this evening."

"How did you realise something was wrong, Doris?" asked the commissioner as he walked into the small living room.

"I walk along path to my room and I see light in guest cottage bathroom, at back. No one sees it from the house. I look and door is open, little bit."

"The door doesn't appear forced. Are any windows open?" The commissioner looked around. Doris walked into the bedroom, whilst Thabiti checked those in the living room. All the windows were latched closed.

"Who had keys for the cottage?" asked the commissioner.

"Not me," said Doris. "I only clean when mistress here. She very secretive."

"When we moved in there were definitely two sets of keys, but I haven't seen either of them," said Thabiti.

"Doris, would you notice the bathroom light in the daytime?" asked Rose.

"All curtains open so the windows light in daytime."

"It looks like our intruder searched today. If they'd called last night, Doris would have noticed the light when she got up this morning. I don't suppose you've had any visitors today, wanted or unwanted?" asked Rose.

Doris replied, "I see no one but guinea fowl make loud noise before lunch. Maybe strange person upset them."

CHAPTER THIRTY-ONE

Thabiti, Rose and Commissioner Akida joined Craig on the veranda at Guinea Fowl Cottage. Rose shook her head at Craig, who appeared to understand her signal to ask no questions at the moment. She would tell him all about someone searching Aisha's guest cottage later.

Rose turned to Thabiti and said, "I'm worried the intruder might return for the laptop. Do you have a safe to lock it in?"

"Do you have a night watchman?" added the commissioner. When Thabiti shook his head, he said, "I could send over a police officer, but they cannot always be trusted to stay awake. Is there anyone you could ask to guard the property tonight?"

"Our casual gardener looks tough and in need of some extra money. I'll call him." Thabiti started to turn away.

The commissioner cleared his throat. "Before you do, there is one final matter, that of your mother's funeral. Did she leave any instructions?"

Thabiti looked down at the floor. "I'd forgotten all about her will, but I'll start looking for it. I hope it wasn't in one of those missing files."

The commissioner continued, "People will expect a grand farewell. You need to think about it over the next few days." Thabiti's shoulders slumped.

"But not tonight," said Rose in a business-like manner.

"I think it's home time, and the business of my supper," announced Craig. "Rose, can you pass my stick?"

Commissioner Akida assisted Craig again as they walked back to their vehicles. Thabiti left to organise a guard and took his mother's laptop with him. Rose was about to get into her Defender when Thabiti and Doris appeared carrying boxes with "Leo's Grocery Store" written on the side of one, and 'Keringet Sparkling Water' on the other.

Thabiti said, "Ma's clothes and things Doris sorted. Please share them with those who need them most, as Ma would have wanted."

"Thank you. It's a kind gesture, and I know many women who'll really appreciate them." Rose opened the rear door of her Defender.

After loading in the boxes, Thabiti asked, "What time shall we meet tomorrow?"

"Shall we say five, outside the casino?"

Thabiti nodded.

Rose added, "Keep safe and sleep well… without the aid of alcohol." Thabiti averted his eyes and Rose guessed he would head straight to the fridge for another beer, or perhaps something stronger after the evening's events.

CHAPTER THIRTY-TWO

O n Wednesday afternoon, Rose spied a free parking space in front of Barclays Bank. She pulled in ahead of a faded yellow Datsun pickup. The bespectacled driver shook a gnarled fist and shouted some choice words.

Rose smiled apologetically, climbed down from her Defender and strode towards the casino, looking around for Thabiti.

It was five o'clock, and many employees had finished work for the day. Several women scrutinised the wares of various stalls huddled together on a vacant patch of roadside land.

There were a few wooden or metal kiosks, but the majority simply comprised wooden tables, with drooping plastic sheets above them, supported by spindly poles.

The stalls were heaped with fruit and vegetables, including large green cabbages, purple-skinned onions, piles of green and red tomatoes, and the local green-skinned lemons.

People who were not shopping were content to find shade under the cover of a metal or concrete shop-canopy, or one of the green-leafed trees which remained in the centre of Nanyuki.

Rose surveyed the entire scene, looking for Thabiti. Would he turn up? Her eyes climbed the imposing Crown Casino. The recently constructed five-storey concrete building towered above its neighbours. She scraped a hand nervously through her curly grey hair, wondering how to gain access and, if successful, where to find the chefs.

Rose walked back up the street. A huddle of three women sat on a wall, surrounded by white plastic bags filled with carrots and potatoes. She wrinkled her nose, overcome by the sickly smell of overripe fruit, and heard a squelch as she stepped on something soft. It was probably a discarded mango skin.

Her foot slipped, and she began to lose her balance until blue-clad arms grasped her.

"Steady, Mama Rose."

"Oh Thabiti, thank you," Rose gasped in relief as she regained her composure. "Where have you been? I thought you were going to leave me to tackle the chefs on my own." She looked at the casino building. "Now you're here, we have to work out how to get in."

Thabiti wore a pair of blue overalls, heavy brown boots and a blue peaked cap. His eyes sparkled with delight as he explained, "Mama Rose, we can go in disguise. And it's great as nobody recognises me in this outfit. I don't feel at all anxious."

Rose looked Thabiti up and down and remarked, "You could easily pass for a delivery man, which gives me an idea. Come back to my car outside Barclays Bank." Rose felt brighter and more positive as a plan formed in her mind.

"Have you had a fruitful day?" she asked.

"Sort of. As you suggested, I stowed Ma's laptop in the safe overnight. When I removed it this morning I accidentally dislodged a piece of vinyl, which covered the bottom of the safe, and hidden beneath it was a brown envelope which contained Ma's will."

"Well done. Did you read it?"

"Of course, I need to find out if she left instructions about her funeral. The commissioner was right about needing to get organised as relatives have been calling all day wanting details of the ceremony. I suspect most are hoping for a handout, or at the very least, free food and accommodation over the funeral.

"You know what traditional funerals are like. The mourning last weeks, and the deceased's family are expected to look after everyone, and slaughter some sheep and goats in the loved one's memory."

Thabiti sighed. "Ma requested a simple cremation, which is a relief, with only very close friends and family. And she expressly ruled out displaying her body in an open coffin, just so folk can file past and check she's really dead. If hordes of relatives want to pay their respects, they can attend a memorial service."

He looked down at the ground. "But where do I start? Can you help me arrange the cremation once we've finished our investigation?"

Rose placed a hand on Thabiti's shoulder. "Of course I'll help you, and so will Craig. Did she leave instructions about her ashes?"

"Yes, and I'll also need your help with that as she wants them released on the hill in the middle of Ol Kilima Ranch."

That surprised Rose. She always thought Aisha wanted to forget her visits to Ol Kilima, as Rose's actions had embarrassed her. Since the shooting incident, Aisha had become distant and their friendship had waned.

Rose said, "Craig has the owner's contact details, although he might not appreciate a call from either Craig or myself. It may be best if you ring him." She paused, and then asked, "Did you discover anything else in your mother's will?" she tried to keep her voice casual, but failed.

"Like who gets her money?" Thabiti grinned.

"Yes. Naturally I'm only asking as it could impact the case."

"Well, she left money to various charities and bequests to a whole host of people I don't know. The remainder of the estate is to be split between myself and Pearl, but to be put in trusts and managed by a trustee. The name of the original trustee has been scored out and replaced with Craig's name. Ma had signed the alteration and dated it at the end of February, so it was a recent change. Do you know if she asked Craig? I do hope he won't mind, but the trustee will receive an annual fee for administering the trust."

"Oh, I'll make certain he doesn't mind, but are you happy with the arrangement?" Rose tilted her head.

"Actually, it's a blessing not having to look after the money, make investments or deal with the tax and legal issues. My needs are quite modest. All I need is money to live on, for my education if I go back to uni, and for any technical equipment I need."

"I wonder how Pearl will take the news," Rose mused.

"She knows, but I'm not sure what she thought. At first she seemed relieved, then upset, but she also appeared worried. I think the investment scheme Francis suggested was one of his, and he won't be thrilled to discover she's not in control of her inheritance."

Thabiti glanced at his blue Captain America watch. "Crikey, it's nearly six!"

"We'd better hurry if we're to speak with the chefs." Rose pulled open the rear door of the Defender to reveal the two boxes of clothes which had been placed inside the previous evening.

"My idea is to carry these into the casino and pretend we're making deliveries." She pulled the right-hand box closer and rotated it. "Look, this one has Leo's Grocery Company printed on it. I'll take some clothes out so it is lighter to carry. And you'd better carry the other box, but make it look heavy as it's supposed to contain bottles of Keringet water."

Thabiti's eyes travelled over Rose. "You can't expect to be allowed in dressed in only jeans and a shirt."

"Ah, yes." She opened the passenger door and rooted around in a green canvas bag in the footwell, from which she removed a white laboratory coat. "I wear this when I assist Dr Emma with animal operations."

Thabiti guided Rose's arms into the coat.

"Thanks. If I follow you, I should be accepted as a delivery man."

Thabiti's good humour faded and his brow furrowed.

"Are you having second thoughts?" Rose asked.

He twisted his watch. "It's just that I'm so used to obeying rules, and Ma's orders were always explicit. It feels strange trying to enter a building without permission."

Rose buttoned up her coat. "Surely not all your computer work is legitimate."

"True. But somehow this is different, more real." Thabiti bit his lip.

"Come on, we're getting nowhere standing here. We'll have to bend a few rules if we're to progress this case. And what's the worst that can happen?

We could be refused entry or thrown out. You know, I've never been ejected from a public place. It might be rather exciting."

"Informing Craig would be less so," muttered Thabiti, but he lifted his box, hoisted it onto his shoulder, and they trooped towards the casino.

CHAPTER THIRTY-THREE

Thabiti walked in front of Rose as they carried their boxes of so-called supplies towards the casino on Wednesday evening. Despite her earlier confidence and bravado, Rose was trembling. What if someone recognised her or stopped them and asked what they were doing?

She knew she was being silly, since casinos were places people visited all the time, even if tonight was a ticket-only event.

The unaccustomed weight of the box on her shoulder was also causing her to shake, and it was growing heavier with each step.

The casino entrance was at the side of the building, as DP Bank occupied the front half of the ground floor. To reach it, they walked under a red and black striped awning, aware of two electricians installing strings of temporary lights.

At the entrance, they were lucky as many people milled around carrying red fabric, crates of beer, and electronic cables. Thabiti plunged forward, followed by Rose holding firmly onto her box.

At the bottom of some concrete stairs, Rose spotted a sign in a silver stand with a large arrow pointing upwards. She struggled as they climbed to the first, and then second floors.

She pulled herself up to the third floor, using the central chrome handrail. With a sigh of relief, she dropped her box to the ground and rubbed her sore shoulder. A chattering group of red-shirted men and women appeared through double black swing doors. With them was a bespectacled man, wearing a black jacket, whose eyes widened when he saw Rose.

"Delivery, kitchen," stammered Thabiti, quickly. Rose lifted her box, which seemed to satisfy the man, and he pointed them to a single black door, located across the lobby from the double swing doors.

"I got us this far, so now it's your turn," Thabiti pronounced, gesturing towards the door.

Rose hesitated. She really didn't know how to approach these men, especially the older one who had been rather disdainful to the commissioner when questioned previously. Still, Thabiti was right, they had made it this far.

Choosing surprise over politeness, Rose entered the kitchen without knocking, and Thabiti followed.

"Evening. I hoped to find you here," she said to the two chefs.

"What do you two want?" the older one scowled.

Rose hesitated.

"Vincent, the boy's just lost his mother, give them a chance." Rose heard Thabiti's intake of breath. Was he offended by being called a boy? Never mind, this was an opening. She moved to one side, so Thabiti could step forward, but the kitchen was long and narrow and there wasn't room for the two of them side by side.

Deftly, she slid behind Thabiti and pushed him forward. "Answer him," she whispered.

"Yes, right. Ma is dead. Yes. And the police won't do anything about it."

"What?" said the younger chef. He stopped filling the miniature pastry cases on the counter and looked over at Thabiti.

Thabiti shrugged. "The local police have been warned off and told to file it as an accidental death, which we don't believe it is. So Mama Rose and I are investigating."

Vincent returned to his chopping board. "You'll get nothing from us. We didn't kill her and we don't know who did. And we don't want to, either."

The kitchen door opened and a cheery middle-aged woman entered, parading a large metal sufuria pan before her. "Scuse me. I need to get in to make the staff food." Rose and Thabiti flattened themselves against the side of the kitchen to allow her access, but Vincent filled the space.

"Oh no, you don't. Management has already increased the number of guests from two hundred to three fifty. And there's not enough room in this broom cupboard as it is. Besides, I'm not having the smell of beans and onions around my food. Go find somewhere else to cook."

The lady's smile vanished. "Where do you expect me to go?"

"I don't know, and I don't care." He pushed the woman back through the entrance and pulled the door closed. As he did so, the sleeve of his chef's jacket rose up his arm, exposing his wrist. He wore a distinctive red and gold watch, with a piece of black tape around the joining of the watch and strap.

Thabiti gasped. "My Ironman watch. Where did you get it?"

Vincent puffed out his chest. "I've no idea what you're talking about. I've had this ages. Look, I had to tape the joining."

"No, you haven't. You just started wearing it this week." The younger chef corrected, but dropped his eyes when Vincent scowled at him.

Thabiti said, "I caught the strap and lost the pin. I left it on the side in the dhobi room to remind me to get it fixed."

"When was that?" asked Rose.

"A few weeks ago. Soon after we moved in, as I caught it carrying a table."

"You're right, now I come to think about it. I presumed it would be thrown out, so I sort of helped myself." Vincent shrugged.

"What else did you sort of help yourself to on Saturday?" Rose asked. Her eyes narrowed. She knew Vincent had been covering something up on Saturday evening.

The younger chef leaned forward and addressed Vincent. "You were stealing? You told me you just wanted to have a look around, as the things people had in their houses fascinated you, and told you something about them."

Vincent glared at him. "Well, they do. Usually that they're rich and won't worry when a few bits and pieces go missing. Are you really that daft? You didn't realise what I was doing? I assumed you were turning a blind eye and waiting to ask me for your cut," said Vincent.

The younger man stared at him, his mouth agape.

"We found the bag you hid in the flower bed." Both chefs turned towards Rose. "There was quite a collection... including keys."

Vincent's arms fell to his side. "I didn't get around to collecting it, not with the police turning up. And there were ambulance men there when I returned on Sunday morning. The keys were a new thing, an impulse I had when I saw them hanging there." He shook himself. "But you've got everything, so no harm done."

Thabiti held out the palm of his hand.

"The watch, of course. I mended it."

Thabiti looked at the tape in repulsion.

"What to do?" mused Rose.

"Ah, you're not going to tell on me to the police, are you? What good would that do?" Vincent raised his arms.

"Very little, I'm afraid," replied Rose. "I regularly visit Nanyuki prison and it's not a pleasant place.

No, I think we can find something else, some community service as it's called." She drew her lips together.

Whilst Rose was thinking, Thabiti interjected, "But who else has he robbed? I bet they haven't got their stuff back. And we've no idea how long he's been playing this game."

"Well," said Rose, lifting her head and catching the sneer Vincent sent in Thabiti's direction. It was quickly replaced with a pleading smile when he realised Rose was watching him.

"We were at Mrs Mutua's last week, and Mr and Mrs Beckett the week before," said the young chef. This time Vincent cuffed his younger colleague over the head, spitting, "Be quiet."

"I think it is prison for you," declared Rose.

"No, no, I have most of the things I took, and I promise to return them."

Vincent gave Rose a puppy dog look.

"I don't believe you, but returning what you can is a start. Take your colleague with you so we can be sure the job's done."

Vincent scowled at Rose.

"Then you can help me with the next four rabies vaccination clinics." This appeared to please the chef.

"And I want a list of all the houses you're working at over the next three months. If I hear that even a loaf of bread has gone missing, I shall make sure everyone in Nanyuki knows you're a thief. I'll discuss the matter with Thabiti very loudly during a busy lunchtime at Dormans. Then see how many people will want you to cook for them in the future."

CHAPTER THIRTY-FOUR

Rose felt elated by her first piece of successful detective work. She and Thabiti stood in the small kitchen on the third floor of the casino, staring at the two chefs from Avocado Catering.

Rose pressed on, taking advantage of the chefs' willingness to talk to her. "We're still looking for a killer. You two were in the kitchen all evening, so did you notice anyone act suspiciously or behaving strangely? Is there anything, when you think back, that doesn't sit quite right in your mind?"

Vincent, the older chef, replied, "We did spend most of our time in the kitchen, as we had a lot of prep work to do. When I look around a property, I tend to make sure nobody is about but I didn't take into account bumping into the main, which shortened my viewing time."

"Is that why you had another look when she went to get changed?" asked the younger chef.

Vincent glared at him. "So what if I did?" He paused and frowned. "The daughter and her boyfriend walked out to the veranda, but the girl returned to her room and I had to hide in the bathroom."

The younger chef added, "And the boyfriend walked back into the house through the kitchen, carrying his clean suit. He told me he'd collected it from his car. Also, Daniel was acting rather odd. He tried to get out of working last Saturday, but nobody else was available. He was irritable when we arrived, stomping around and snapping at us when we gave him jobs to do. But later on he seemed jumpy and nervous, but kind of excited at the same time."

"You're right," said Vincent, suddenly willing to help. He added, "He wouldn't be still, even when carrying the platters, and I was sure he'd drop one. He also had a gleam to his skin, so I suspected he'd taken something and was on a high."

"Mind you, that all stopped when he found the body. The colour drained from his face," noted the younger chef.

"Could he have killed my Ma?" asked Thabiti.

"I wouldn't think so, but you never know. I gather there was a bit of history between them. By the way, he seems pretty pleased with himself tonight," said Vincent.

"He's working here tonight?" Rose asked, her eyes widening.

"Yes. But where's he got to? He only went to collect some bowls from the van, and that must have been twenty minutes ago. The idle blighter. I'll have something to say to him when he gets back. Now we must get cracking. The VIP guests are already arriving and they'll be wanting something to eat soon." Vincent returned to a green plastic chopping board and picked up his knife.

"Remember, I want confirmation that you've returned the items you stole, and I'll be in touch about assisting me with my rabies clinics," Rose promised.

As she and Thabiti turned to leave, Vincent waved the knife. He called, "Yeah, yeah, and you can take your boxes with you."

Rose and Thabiti left the compact casino kitchen and walked straight into Pearl as she emerged from the adjacent ladies' toilet.

Whilst she looked stunning in a shimmering black dress, with a short matching jacket and clutch purse, she appeared flustered and there was a red mark on her arm.

She rubbed her eyes when she saw them. "Goodness, what are you two doing here? And why are you dressed so strangely?"

Thabiti tapped his nose and responded, "Just a little snooping, but we're leaving now. Have a pleasant party."

Rose didn't move. "Where's Francis? Is with you this evening?"

"He's upstairs, having arrived early for a meeting. But he seems to be enjoying himself, mingling with influential people, especially those from Nairobi." Pearl rubbed the back of her neck. "I must join him. Night." She fled, her heels clacking on the concrete stairs.

The entrance hall was noisy and busy and Rose and Thabiti were relieved not to be recognised. As Rose removed her white coat in the shadows of an alley outside the entrance, she became aware that all was not right. She heard shouts and ladies screaming. Rose and Thabiti abandoned their boxes and ran to the front of DP Bank.

The street was a melee. Guests queuing under the awning, waiting for the casino to open, tried to push their way back to the road but were hampered by the arrival of new guests. More people waited outside the bank, while others were getting out of cars. Rose saw that between her and her parked Land Rover, there was a growing mass of people.

"It can't be a car accident," noted Thabiti. "There's not enough room. Perhaps someone was hit by a boda-boda."

Rose heard the wail of police sirens before she saw blue flashing lights. The first car sped along the main highway and squealed around the turning to Barclays Bank. It parked across the road at the far side of the gathering crowd.

A second car was making its sluggish journey through the throng of people in front of Rose and Thabiti. Rose grabbed Thabiti's arm, and they pushed past casino guests to the rear of the police car, and followed its slow journey towards the centre of the excitement.

The commissioner stepped out of the furthest police car, still fastening buttons on his best blue uniform. As he struggled to make headway through the mass of people, a young policewoman ran after him, waving his cap.

A police Land Cruiser arrived and officers jumped out of the back and rushed to the scene, where they began roughly pushing the crowd back. Other officers abandoned the car which Rose and Thabiti were following and also began clearing the throng of people. Rose and Thabiti held their ground.

The commissioner disappeared from view, but as the crowd dispersed, Rose saw him squatting by a heap on the ground. He stood, removed his cap, and ran his hand through his hair. He looked towards the casino roof and back at the people still gathered alongside DP Bank.

He caught sight of Rose and gestured for her to join him. The final stragglers were escorted away and two policemen arrived with a black tarpaulin.

"Just a minute," ordered the commissioner. He turned to Rose and Thabiti and said solemnly, "Daniel, the waiter."

Rose focused on the heap on the road, which took on the proportions of a body. The limbs were splayed unnaturally and a trickle of blood seeped from the left ear.

"What happened? Was he knocked over?" asked Thabiti.

"No, he fell from the casino. I've sent officers to speak to witnesses, but there are no balconies and I can't see any open windows. Can you?"

Rose and Thabiti looked up the outside of the building.

"No, which I presume means he fell, tripped or slipped off the roof," noted Rose.

"Or jumped," added Thabiti.

"Or he was pushed," said the commissioner gravely. "Impossible to say which at the moment, from the state and position of his body."

Rose shook her head. "I can't believe he jumped. He gave me the impression that his life was improving."

"And why would he be on the roof? The chefs sent him to get something out of their van, which is parked on the roadside behind us," said Thabiti.

"What had he got himself mixed up with?" The commissioner was solemn, rigid, with his head bowed and he held his cap by his side. "Did you two see anything? Or were you still questioning the chefs inside the casino?"

Rose replied in a flat, monotone voice, "We were, and we only realised something had happened when we left the building. Poor boy. Whatever he was up to, he didn't deserve this."

"No, foolish as he might be, this is a tragic end."

The commissioner nodded to his colleagues, who covered Daniel's body with the tarpaulin.

CHAPTER THIRTY-FIVE

Outside the casino on Wednesday evening, Rose, Thabiti and Commissioner Akida turned away from Daniel's dead body, which had been covered with a black tarpaulin. The bespectacled man from the casino rushed towards them, but his mouth fell open as he looked from Rose to Thabiti to the commissioner and back to Rose.

"Yes?" said the commissioner.

"Commissioner, what's happening? Your officers won't let the guests into the casino and my staff are corralled on the third floor. This is opening night!"

"Sir, a waiter has fallen from the building. We need to establish where he fell from before we can allow anyone in or out." The commissioner turned to Rose and Thabiti, who stood behind him, and whispered, "Now we're in trouble."

Hurrying towards them was a thin man with a beaked nose and a nasal voice. "This won't do, Commissioner. The governor is to deliver a speech to the guests in ten minutes. You must allow the casino to open."

"Evening, Gregory. As I was telling this gentleman, a man fell from the building, and we need to confirm where from before anyone else moves in, out, or around the casino."

Rose observed the building and the faces peering down from the third and fourth floor windows. From an open window on the fourth floor, a voice shouted, "Get on with it, Gregory."

The third person to approach the commissioner was the young policewoman Rose had spotted earlier, waving the commissioner's cap. The commissioner turned his back on the two men to speak with her, Rose and Thabiti.

The policewoman said, "Sir, there are no windows on this side of the building that open wide enough for a man to climb out of. But the roof is flat and only surrounded by a low parapet wall. It was too dark up there to see much else."

"Well done, Constable Wachira. We might as well let the guests in. At least that will appease the governor. Can you ask Mutua to guard the stairs to the roof, as I don't want anyone up there tonight. Have we taken names and contact details from everyone inside?"

"Staff, yes. The VIP guests on the 4th floor weren't very cooperative, but we found the guest list which made it easier."

"Good work." The commissioner turned back to the two men and said, "The guests may enter once they have answered a few questions from my officers. Hopefully, some of them witnessed the fall. I am afraid the governor will still be able to make his address."

The man called Gregory snorted at the commissioner's sarcasm and strode away.

The commissioner addressed the bespectacled man. "I presume you are the manager." The man nodded. "Then you are a waiter short for tonight. Take my friend Thabiti here and find him something suitable to wear."

Realising that Thabiti was about to protest, he said to him, "I need someone who isn't a police officer to be my eyes and ears amongst staff and guests. Don't worry, nobody will recognise you. This lot," he gestured with an outstretched hand, "will be far too preoccupied with themselves, the excitement of somebody falling from the casino, and free food and drink. They will not be concerned about a waiter."

He turned to Rose. "Would you be willing to go to the party?"

"She can't go in dressed like that," protested the manager.

"Don't worry, I have an idea," said Rose.

"Good, I would like you up in the VIP area... as my guest. Take my ticket and I'll meet you there. I need to sort out a few things with this gentleman."

Rose followed the two men, but turned down the alley beside the casino entrance. She found the boxes of Aisha's clothes that she and Thabiti had left. She hoped to find something suitable in them to wear for the event and prayed it would fit, as Aisha had filled out over the years.

With only limited light from the entrance, it was hard to see what clothes there were. As she held up each item, she knew her behaviour would look suspicious to anyone who spotted her.

In the second box, which Thabiti had carried, she found a wrap-around kanga skirt, which fitted her when she pulled it tight over her jeans. With her back to the casino, she removed her shirt and replaced it with a white one which she had found.

Finally, she slipped on a pair of ballet pumps, which were a size too large, and wrapped a green scarf around her shoulders.

She hoped this mismatch of oversized clothing would allow her to enter the casino.

She bundled her clothes, and the rest of Aisha's, back into the boxes. She tapped out a quick text message to Craig, praying he wouldn't be too agitated by the turn of events, and placed her phone and car keys in the small black clutch bag she'd found, which was similar to the one Pearl had been carrying.

She walked confidently up to the entrance, presented the commissioner's invitation, and entered the casino.

CHAPTER THIRTY-SIX

Rose picked her way to the 4th floor VIP area of the new casino, being careful not to lose her oversized shoes. At the double doors, she took a deep breath and entered in what she hoped was an elegant manner. The room had a deep red carpet, mahogany-coloured wall panels and gold light fittings.

To the left was a bar and light danced across the chrome counter. There were four gaming tables, glass-topped with green gaming mats, surrounded by comfortable leather chairs. Excited men and women filled most of the seats, whilst others peered over their shoulders, enjoying the fun without taking the risk.

Few people appeared to notice Rose's entry, but a solitary black-clad figure looked up from where she sat on a barstool. Rose walked across to join Pearl, who she realised must be confused by her unexpected appearances and strange outfits. It was true. Pearl gaped at her and eventually asked, "Are those Ma's clothes?"

"I had nothing else to wear. There's been a terrible accident. Daniel, the waiter from Dormans, who was at your mother's party, has been killed."

Pearl was silent. She frowned. "Oh, dear. Is that why there was such a crowd on the street earlier? Someone said a man had jumped off the roof. Was that Daniel?" She uncrossed and re-crossed her legs.

"Yes, but I don't believe he jumped, which means he either fell or was pushed. If he was pushed, his death could be linked to your mother's."

Pearl leaned back, tapping her fingers on her thigh. "But why are you and Thabiti here? I spotted him working as a waiter."

"The commissioner asked us to stay, and listen to what people were saying about the accident."

"I can't see how anyone in here can help. When did it happen?" asked Pearl.

"While Thabiti and I were still in the building, so probably just before we bumped into you. I'm not sure of the exact time."

"So when the VIP guests were arriving. I don't see how any of them could be involved, and the other guests weren't due to arrive until seven. Daniel must have sneaked up onto the roof, tripped and fallen off. Poor soul." Pearl sipped a vivid orange cocktail.

"Have you seen anyone who seemed flustered, out of breath, or excited?"

Pearl laughed. "Well, yes, all those at the gaming tables. They've had lots of free alcohol and they keep slapping each other on the shoulder and telling jokes in loud voices."

Rose looked at the men and women at the nearest table. Their faces were flushed as they laughed loudly, seemingly oblivious to the tragedy that had occurred.

She glimpsed Francis at a farther table, with his arm around a young woman. Rose decided to change tack while she had Pearl on her own. "I heard Thabiti found your Mother's will today."

"Yes, it's such a relief she didn't want a traditional funeral. I'm not sure we could have coped with hosts of relatives pretending to feel sorry for us. I guess that's why she left bequests to so many people."

"And what provision did the will make for you?" pried Rose.

They were interrupted before Pearl could respond.

"Pearl, this is where you're hiding. I've had a great run at the table."

Francis picked up Rose's bag, grabbed a handful of gaming chips from his pocket, and stuffed them into it, likely mistaking it for Pearl's bag. Gone was the hesitancy and preoccupation of the evening before.

Here was a man brimming with confidence and at ease with his peers, although there was a sheen of sweat across his forehead.

"But you said you don't agree with gambling?" Remarked Rose.

"It's just a bit of fun, no harm in it. Did I overhear you say something about your Ma's will? Has it been found?" he asked, jittering a foot on the ground.

"Thabiti found it hidden under something in the safe." Pearl swirled her drink.

"So when can you expect to be a lady of fortune?" Francis's eyes sparkled.

Pearl looked at Francis with a bittersweet smile. "No time soon. The money is to be controlled for me, bound up in a trust. Ma never trusted me." She swallowed a large mouthful of orange liquid.

Francis patted Pearl on the head. "Never mind." He looked up to see the young woman from the gaming table pass. Jumping up, he led her back to the table, mouth close to her ear as he whispered something that they both laughed at.

He did not look back at Rose or Pearl.

Pearl picked at the material of her bag. "That's the President's niece. Even after all I've done, I doubt he'll be interested in me now." Her chin trembled. "I think I'll say some goodbyes and find Thabiti, and see if he wants to go home."

"What about the chips Francis gave me?" Rose opened her black bag.

"You keep them." Pearl smiled sadly and walked across to a gaming table.

CHAPTER THIRTY-SEVEN

Commissioner Akida joined Rose at the 4th floor bar at the casino on Wednesday evening and asked, "Is all not well with our golden couple?"

Rose replied, "It seems not. Francis is ambitious and egotistical. He's just heard Pearl won't have control of her inheritance and already seems to be moving on to the next dazzling prospect. This one is very well connected, the President's niece."

"He needs to be careful then and treat her properly. I hope young Pearl doesn't do something she later regrets." The commissioner surveyed the gaming tables.

"She might appear glamorous, but underneath, she's rather vulnerable and naïve. Aisha seems to have been rather controlling." Rose's legs felt heavy.

"I think we could both do with a drink after tonight's events. What would you like?" the commissioner asked.

"I have to drive home," sighed Rose.

"Don't worry, I'll ask Constable Wachira to take you."

As Rose settled down with a large glass of white wine, Thabiti appeared carrying trays of sausage rolls, savoury tarts and mini Yorkshire puddings filled with roast beef. He placed the trays on a table and sat down.

"Where's the VIP doorman?" he mumbled through a Yorkshire pudding.

"No idea. I walked straight in," replied Rose.

"It was our man mountain of a barman from Ma's party. He was talking with Constable Wachira and looked right through me, but his cheek twitched, so I'm sure he recognised me. I wonder where he is now?" Thabiti looked around.

"What else have you found out?" asked the commissioner.

Thabiti's gaze returned to Rose and the commissioner. "A member of the casino staff saw Daniel standing at the bottom of the small staircase that leads to the roof. He couldn't see who Daniel was speaking to, as the other person was standing around the corner. The voice was high-pitched, and the words spoken quickly, so he couldn't be sure if it was a man or woman."

"What time was this?" asked the commissioner.

"As the VIP guests were arriving, so around half six." Thabiti's eyes strayed back to the gaming tables. "Have my sister and Francis had a bust up? Francis seems to be getting friendly with another girl."

"The President's niece. He was already with her when I arrived, and then he heard about the will, and that Pearl won't have control of her money, and he returned to the girl."

"Poor Pearl," sigh Thabiti. "I'll go over in a minute and see if she wants to go home."

Rose picked up her bag. "Francis mistakenly gave me some of his gambling chips. He put a handful in this bag of your mother's that I borrowed." Rose shook it.

"Good for you. So those are some of Ma's clothes? No wonder they're far too big." Thabiti grinned.

"Commissioner," Rose was serious again. "Where do we go from here?"

"Nobody can stop me from investigating Daniel's death, and if he was pushed, it is likely to be connected with Aisha. At least that's my opinion. I still cannot actively look into her death, but…"

Rose felt weary. As the adrenaline and excitement of the night's events receded, so did her energy. She needed to escape, to be home.

"Are we responsible for Daniel's death?" Rose pulled at her kanga skirt. "If someone paid him to kill Aisha and has now silenced him, it could be our fault for asking him questions."

Commissioner Akida turned to Rose and replied, "How could it be your fault? Sure, you asked him a few questions in a coffee shop, but there was no confession and no hint of his involvement in Aisha's death. I think we should call it a night. I'll fetch Constable Wachira, but I would like to examine the roof tomorrow. One of my men will be guarding access tonight... if he stays awake and sober. Would you both join me in the morning? Shall we say ten o'clock downstairs?"

Pearl approached them as they stood up. "Can we go home?" she asked Thabiti in a weary voice, as a tear slid down her cheek.

CHAPTER THIRTY-EIGHT

R ose slept fitfully and did not feel refreshed on Thursday morning. Exhausted from the events at the casino, she had fallen straight to sleep, but woke at half-past three with the sound of a woman screaming inside her head.

She presumed she finally dozed off at five, but woke with the morning light at quarter past six.

At the breakfast table she could feel Craig's stares as he spooned porridge into his mouth. She concentrated on her own breakfast of fruit salad and natural yoghurt, with a spoonful of Uhuru honey and a handful of chopped nuts and seeds.

She hoped this would energise her for the day ahead.

"Rose, are you going to enlighten me about last night's events? That young policewoman said there had been another death, and that someone had fallen from the casino roof. You weren't able to tell me anything last night, and you looked rather odd in that long kanga skirt and oversized shirt."

She put down her spoon. "Craig, I'm worried it's my fault he died. If I hadn't started nosing around and asking questions, he might still be alive."

"Who might be?" Craig asked as he picked up his coffee cup.

"Young Daniel, the waiter from Dormans."

"He fell from the roof? How did that happen?" Craig drank his coffee.

"I don't know. The police presume it was the roof, but it was too dark to look last night. Poor boy, lying in a heap on the road." Craig finished his coffee and reached for a piece of toast.

Rose's stomach turned as she looked down at her fruit salad, so she pushed it away.

"Eat up. You need your strength, old girl, if you're going to continue this investigation."

Rose raised her hands, palm up. "That's the trouble. Should I continue? I feel I'm doing more harm than good. Maybe it's best to let matters be, as we have no idea of the consequences if I continue."

"True, but you can only act with the facts you have at hand. None of us can predict the future."

Rose yawned. Her eyes twitched, and her head felt dull. She wondered if she could curl up back in bed.

Craig chose marmalade to spread on his toast. "You're a person of action. You always have been, and not someone who hides away. You weigh up the options and decide what action to take."

"And if that action leads to someone's death?" Rose's hands tightened into fists.

"Rose, are we talking about Aisha's case, or the poacher incident on Ol Kilima?" Craig cut his toast in half and lifted a piece to his mouth.

"Well, it's the same thing. Can I trust my own judgment?" She ran a hand through her hair.

Craig swallowed. "OK, take this business with Aisha and Daniel. You seem to think the two deaths are connected. That your questioning Daniel, to find out about Aisha, caused his death, but it sounds like Daniel was already mixed up in the case. I don't believe your interview would have distressed him to the point of jumping from the roof. Nor would it have worried another party enough to kill him."

Rose stared at the empty stone bird table. "He was my lead suspect, as I thought someone had exploited his grudge against Aisha for being wrongly accused of stealing. On Saturday evening, he frequently visited the tent, so had ample opportunity to commit the crime. He was also the one who discovered the body."

Craig tapped his fingers. "Is it possible he killed Aisha on his own initiative? If so, where did the money come from to buy the watch, belt and other expensive items?"

Rose put her elbow on the table and rested her chin against her fist. "So it appears Daniel was also a victim. A victim of someone with money, who had their own reason for wanting Aisha dead."

Craig continued drumming his fingers. "Of course, it could be as simple as blackmail. If Daniel walked back and forth between the house and the tent, he might have seen someone else kill Aisha and demanded money for his silence."

"That fits," replied Rose. "I doubt Daniel would have told the police if he had seen anything. Maybe he was greedy and threatened the actual killer. They could have arranged to meet him on the roof and pushed him off, thereby solving their problem."

Rose reached for her breakfast and ate a spoonful of fruit and yoghurt.

"See, you're better already. You've some colour in your cheeks and your appetite's returned. So, whilst I would prefer you sit here with me and finish a crossword, I expect you need to solve this puzzle. If you want to appease your conscience about Daniel's death, and continue your investigation into Aisha's, I suggest you 'follow the money', as the saying goes. Where had Daniel's newfound wealth come from?"

Rose poured herself a fresh cup of tea.

Craig was right.

However upset she was, she wouldn't be satisfied until she knew why Aisha was killed. She would have to continue… but make sure nobody else died.

CHAPTER THIRTY-NINE

R ose and Craig were finishing breakfast on Thursday morning when Kipto opened the door onto the patio. "There's a man at the gate. All puff up like a cockerel. Says he needs to talk with you, Mama Rose. Says he's 'the grandson'."

Rose's hands shook, and she set her cup down before she spilt her tea.

Craig sighed. "Obviously, a day to confront our troubles. Don't worry, Rose, this time I am here. Show him in, Kipto."

Rose and Craig moved from their old wooden outdoor dining table to the cedar chairs. Rose gripped her cup tightly, taking small sips of tea.

Neither of them stood when the young man appeared and sat opposite them on the large wooden sofa.

He looked around him, out into the garden and beyond to Mount Kenya, whose snow-covered peak shone in the morning sunshine. "Fine view. Fine place you have here."

"What can I do for you?" asked Craig. His expression was stony.

"No offer of chai? Oh, well, it's your wife I've come to see." The grandson stared at Rose.

"I speak for my wife. You can tell me what you want."

The young man shifted his gaze to Craig. "If that's the way you want it, let's get down to business. We know your wife shot and killed my grandfather. You see, my family is poor. We live in a tin mabati hut and are often hungry, but you have this fine house with plenty to eat."

The grandson raised one arm, palm upwards, and gestured around him. "It's only fair you share some of this with us, with me."

"And if we don't?" Craig crossed his arms.

"Come, there's no need to be like that... but the longer I stay in Nanyuki, waiting for what I'm owed, the more people I meet and talk to about why I'm here. That's not good for your wife's respectability and her job."

"Now look here, don't you threaten us!" Craig spluttered.

Rose placed her cup on a small table and reached over to touch Craig on the shoulder. Meeting and holding the gaze of her adversary, she said, "Very well, what is it you want? Money, I presume."

"Nothing can be done for my grandfather or father, as both have passed away, but I'd like to make something of myself... for their benefit." He puffed out his chest. "I want four million shillings."

Craig pulled away from Rose's hand and his body tensed. "Four million? Where can we get that kind of money?"

"This house must be worth a bit?" The grandson smirked.

"Probably, but it's not ours. We rent it. I'm retired and Rose works in the community. And we don't have that kind of money."

The man sneered at them and leaned forward. "Well, speak to some of your rich friends. Otherwise, it won't be just your reputation that's damaged. And, yes, I am threatening you." He stood and looked down at them. "I need some funds to be going on with. Shall we say five thousand shillings?"

Rose's mouth was dry, and she thought it best to comply. The man rubbed his neck and a sheen of sweet was visible on his cheeks and forehead. She stood and walked to her bedroom, making sure he had not followed her, and raided her emergency fund. Shame there was only ten thousand shillings there, not four million.

"Most kind," he said, closing his palm over the thousand shilling notes. "Shall we say a further deposit in three days? One hundred thousand this time."

"Don't be ridiculous," exclaimed Craig.

The man ignored him, but smiled menacingly at Rose and left. She collapsed in her chair as blood deserted her body, leaving her cold. Kipto peered around the door.

"Make sure that man has left and don't let him back in," Craig snapped.

"Tea, please," whispered Rose.

Rose and Craig sat in silence while Kipto brought a fresh cup of tea for Rose and cleared away the remains of breakfast.

Rose clasped her cup and took grateful sips, feeling the warmth penetrate her body. "Craig, what are we going to do?"

"What can we do? We don't have that amount of money and neither do our friends, at least not readily available."

Craig tilted his head. "What do we really know about him? He claims to be the dead poacher's grandson, but we have no proof he really is. We need to find out more about him."

Rose sagged, and the tea turned sour in her mouth.

"Please don't get upset," said Craig. "You have enough to deal with. But I still have contacts out in the Laikipia bush, so I'll see what I can find out about the man."

Rose's phone rang.

CHAPTER FORTY

After breakfast on Thursday morning, Rose turned her red Land Rover Defender off the tarmacked highway onto a dirt track leading to the North Kenya Polo Club. Clouds of dust flew behind her as she sped down the hill.

The call she received, after the grandson's visit, was from a groom looking after polo ponies stabled at the club. Having been unable to contact his employer, who was on safari in Tanzania, he called Rose.

Craig had come with her so he could attend a committee meeting at the Polo Club later in the morning.

Craig's hand once again shot up to seize the grab handle. The car launched over a large hump in the road and jolted as it landed back on the track and sped forward.

"Rose!" Craig roared, but knowing that a horse's life depended on her, Rose flew on.

North Kenya Polo Club was located on the northern slope of Mount Kenya, over eight thousand feet above sea level. It was reached by driving north from Nanyuki, up through the foothills and some of the most productive farming land in the world.

Had it not been for the spawning of a shanty village on its boundary, where houses had appeared like fungal hyphae over the past two years, Rose believed it would be the most beautiful club in the world. The mountain towered above it on one side and the vast bush country of northern Kenya fell away on the other.

Rose had been consulted about an increasing number of impaction colics during the past few weeks. Horses like to roam in fields rather than remain in their stables all day, but the lack of rain, harshness of the sun and overgrazing of the Polo Club paddocks had stripped them bare of grass.

The grooms, known as syces, were substituting grass with hay for the horses to eat, which they placed in piles on the ground. As the horses nibbled at the last stalks of hay they ingested tiny stones and small amounts of soil and sand, which accumulated in their colons, causing obstructions. If left untreated, the horse could die.

Rose threw the steering wheel right and simultaneously stamped on the brake as they came to a jarring halt by a black metal, five-bar gate. A wooden carved sign with North Kenya Polo Club dangled down from the gate.

Craig snorted. Rose hoped this was because of the damaged sign and not her driving. She completed the time-consuming task of getting in and out of the car to open and close the gate. She drove through a conifer coppice at a steadier pace, past the wooden stable block and along the track adjacent to the polo pitch.

She parked as close as she could to the wooden clubhouse and was met by the club groundsman, who rushed down the clubhouse steps to help

Craig out of the car. Rose reversed and sped back to the polo stables.

Her patient was standing between two rows of wooden clapboard stables, surrounded by syces concerned for its wellbeing, but relieved it wasn't one of their charges. The mare bowed her head as she pawed at the ground with a front leg and then kicked at her belly.

Rose jumped from her car just as the horse bent its legs. "Don't let her lie down and roll. Quick, walk her forward. Rolling can twist her gut and I don't have the equipment to operate here." Rose removed a hypodermic needle and a small glass bottle from her medical bag. "First, I'll inject her with Flunixin to ease her pain."

From the back of her car, Rose removed five plastic bottles labelled 'liquid paraffin', a piece of clear plastic rubber hose and a white plastic funnel. She attached one end of the hose to the funnel and stepped towards the horse.

She was pleased there were lots of syces standing around, as they could help her. "You two, hold each side of the mare's head. Careful now, she's in pain and could still panic. Good girl."

Rose patted the horse's neck and pushed against the corner of her mouth. It opened wide enough for Rose to feed the free end of the pipe down her throat.

The descending pipe created a bulge down the left-hand side of the neck, so Rose knew it was in the correct place and heading to the stomach, rather than the lungs. Pouring liquid into the lungs would be a sure way to kill the horse.

"Hold this," she said to the wide-eyed syce. She opened a bottle of liquid paraffin, held the funnel above the height of the horse's mouth, and poured the paraffin into it.

A few syces had seen her conduct this procedure before and they nudged each other, laughing at their wide-eyed colleagues. "I'm doing this to try to clear the blockage. The paraffin lubricates around it and will hopefully loosen some sand, soil and retained faeces." In total, she poured five litres of paraffin into the mare.

Paraffin was not guaranteed to move the obstruction, so she decided to give the horse an enema as well. She asked for a bucket into which she mixed a litre of water, a cup of olive oil and a cup of washing up liquid.

She pulled a long, blue latex glove onto her arm, filled a large syringe with the mixture, and pushed it, and her hand, into the horse's rectum and squeezed. She repeated the process until all the liquid had been used up.

She said to the horse's syce, "See if she will walk now."

The mare refused to move but occasionally reached round with her head to look at her flank. Rose felt like a magician. Her audience waited in unaccustomed silence to see what trick she would perform next. She decided to try one more treatment. It was one she had devised herself.

She opened a can of Tusker beer into which she grated a dessertspoon-sized portion of fresh ginger. Her spectators stepped closer to watch this piece of sorcery. Once again, she put her hand into the mare's mouth and tipped the contents of the can down the horse's throat.

"That's all I can do for now. Don't let her roll, but encourage her to walk, as it will help loosen the obstruction. I'll be back soon."

Rose drove back to the clubhouse, where the committee meeting had started. They were discussing such dry subjects as whether the standard measure for spirits at the club bar should be single or double. She retreated outside and called Commissioner Akida.

"Rose, thank you for your message. How is your patient?"

"Comfortable and alive... for now, Commissioner."

"Good, good. Thabiti and I examined the casino roof."

CHAPTER FORTY-ONE

"I t's a shame Mama Rose is not here, but I know sick animals cannot wait." The commissioner and Thabiti stood on the flat roof of the casino, looking out over Nanyuki town.

"Much has changed since I first arrived here as a young sergeant. Back then, all the buildings were single-storey, but I can see at least ten others the same height as this one. And over there is what looks like a block of flats being built, which will be even taller."

Wow, thought Thabiti. Nanyuki had seemed a sleepy, insignificant town after Nairobi, but now he could see buildings spread out in all directions.

At the edge of the town, toward Mount Kenya, was an empty piece of bush land.

The commissioner followed his gaze. "There was an entire shanty town on that land at one stage, but it belongs to the Kenyan Army and they cleared it when they upgraded their security arrangements."

Despite the previous evening's events, or perhaps because of them, Thabiti was awake and refreshed. He had taken Pearl home with him from the casino.

She had returned to being the young, vulnerable girl he remembered, and he'd hugged her as her shoulders shook and the tears flowed. She told him she had thought Francis was the one as he had been so attentive and caring, but now it looked as if he was only interested in her money... and after all she had done for him. Thabiti was worried. Just what had she done for Francis?

Commissioner Akida interrupted his musings. "You know that chef from Avocado Catering, the older, shorter one? He was in my office this morning making a scene. Apparently Daniel was sent to fetch something from the van, but as he did not return, they do not have the keys. They were not in Daniel's pockets, so see if you can spot them up here."

Thabiti looked around the concrete flat roof. The building contractors had left a lot of rubbish, but the small mounds of gravel and dusty cement would be washed away when the rains arrived.

"It looks like someone comes up here for a break." Thabiti moved a red Lay's crisp packet with his foot and spotted an empty Fanta Orange can a few feet away. "Those planks and crates have been moved to create benches." He looked around and asked, "Where would Daniel have fallen from?"

They picked their way to the edge of the roof facing the road. As the constable had told them, there was a small concrete parapet wall, but nothing else to prevent someone from falling... or being pushed. Thabiti shivered and stepped back.

How could he tell how many people had been on the roof or when they had been there? He had hoped to find scrape marks indicating that

Daniel's body had been moved, but there was nothing.

"Daniel could have come up here last night for a break, or to look around, and in the dusky light simply fallen or tripped."

The commissioner echoed Thabiti's thoughts. "Impossible to say what happened."

After his meeting with Daniel and Mama Rose in Dormans, Thabiti couldn't believe Daniel had jumped. Fallen maybe, but most likely someone had pushed him.

Light reflected off a small object at Thabiti's feet. He bent down to pick it up, feeling his tummy tighten. It was a pearl earring. He also spotted a set of keys in the shadow of the parapet wall. Placing his foot over the earring, he reached for the keys and held them up.

In a squeaky voice, he said, "Avocado Catering. I guess these are the missing keys." A small gold disk fell into his hand as Commissioner Akida took the keys. Whilst the commissioner was distracted, Thabiti picked up the earring and pocketed it together with the disc.

"Well done. At least that's one mystery solved," said the commissioner. "Let's go down and see if Constable Wachira has found out anything else."

Thabiti followed the commissioner with the earring in his pocket weighing him down. Pearl owned a set which to his untrained eye looked the same or very similar. Pearl's words came back to him. What had she done for Francis? He should have handed the earring over, but he couldn't bring himself to do it.

He needed to consult Mama Rose.

CHAPTER FORTY-TWO

Rose was disappointed by the commissioner's news, but not entirely surprised at the lack of evidence at the casino. At least the presence of the van keys proved Daniel had been on the roof and, so it followed, had fallen from it. She was sure his death was linked with Aisha's, but if it was, it just raised more questions.

Then there was the greedy grandson. What had caused him to look for her now? And Craig was right. Was he the man he claimed to be? If so, it was likely life had treated him harshly, or at least his father and grandmother, who had to support themselves. Still, Rose reflected, the grandfather was not entirely blameless.

Rose had begun to remember long-buried details about the shooting incident and its aftermath. Poachers usually steered clear of houses and farm compounds, preferring the cover of the savannah, where they were less likely to be discovered.

They were not hunting for food but to make money from the skins and ivory of the animals they killed. This gang had chosen to enter the Ol Kilima farm compound.

Rose remembered seeing the group of men walk into the farmyard and as she closed and bolted the back door, she heard them shout "bring her out". Aisha and Rose had no idea who the *her* was, but, frightened, they had hidden in the kitchen pantry with the house girl.

Rose had no notion what had made her leave her refuge and run to Craig's study. Perhaps it was her underlying need for action, and not accept her fate without fighting back. Or perhaps it was some instinct to protect herself and her friend.

She and Craig had occasionally shot at tins on the garden wall. She knew he kept his gun in the study and once she found the cartridges, she loaded the gun. She had no intention of hurting anyone, and the gun was only for protection, as a deterrent to warn the men to keep away from Aisha and herself.

In the kitchen, the chanting sounded louder. She couldn't see the men and daren't open the back door. She had pointed the gun out of the kitchen window, which overlooked the garden. A man spotted it and called to his friends. She heard frantic shouts and running footsteps, and in her panic, she pulled the trigger.

When Craig returned home, he had found her, Aisha, and the house girl still hiding in the pantry. There was some blood by the yard wall, but no dead body. She was arrested a week later, but neither she nor Craig saw the corpse of the man she was accused of killing.

After the incident, Aisha returned to Nairobi and Craig reluctantly left Rose alone to attend meetings in Nanyuki.

One morning a police Land Cruiser, from Rumuruti, drove into the yard and two stony faced officers grabbed her wrist and bundled her into the back of their vehicle. The first night had been the worst.

Dressed only in jodhpurs and a short-sleeved T-shirt from riding her horse, she had shivered from fright and cold on the bare concrete floor.

The next day, a pair of intimidating officers questioned her, or rather barraged her with accusations. At least they hadn't hit her, although they had threatened to.

She remembered cowering when a large policewoman approached, holding her baton aloft with a gleam of malice in her eyes. But someone had entered the room, Rose could not recall who, and the blow was not delivered.

By mid-afternoon, she'd had no food or water and the temperature inside the tinned roof interrogation room had reached an unbearable temperature. These factors, combined with a lack of sleep, had led her to accept the officers' version of events.

A flustered Craig arrived in the afternoon bringing much-needed supplies of spare clothes, a mattress and bedding, and fresh water and food to supplement the police's meagre offerings.

She had been left alone in her concrete cell for the rest of the day and the following morning, with only the occasional taunt shouted through the small barred window, usually by police officers.

Aisha arrived on the third day. Rose had a vague memory of Aisha's father standing outside the interview room arguing with a senior policeman, but Aisha had never mentioned his involvement.

Aisha returned to Nairobi, promising to help Rose. But why Nairobi? What had Aisha been able to achieve there that she could not in Rumuruti? Whatever it was had worked, as Rose was released on the seventh day of her imprisonment. She remembered her utter despair, believing she was being transferred to Nanyuki prison as the fat policewoman had sneered at her.

The charges had been dropped, but the stigma remained. And her own conscience? She had taken a life, and that was a sin, the gravest sin of all, and for that the Lord would punish her. And she had been punished.

Craig had lost his job and, as a result, they had lost their home. Begging and borrowing, they had been lent a run-down cottage on a farm outside Nanyuki.

She knew Craig blamed himself for being away when the poachers invaded the farm complex and he began to drink as a way to cope with the shame and guilt. Rose understood, but it made her life harder.

Still, she had found the new simplicity of life calming. It allowed her to recover from the ordeal of imprisonment and police interrogation. She had dug out and planted a small garden with vegetables, begged a few chickens and a goat from friends, and shot rabbits for meat. Then there had been the birth of her daughter, Heather.

As a family, they worked hard until they were back on their feet. She helped with sick and injured animals on the farms and villages around her, and gradually her knowledge, experience and following grew. Then Craig had been given a farm manager's job, and they had built a steady and respectable life for themselves.

The deterioration in her friendship with Aisha was her main regret. Aisha appeared to distance herself deliberately from them.

She had stopped visiting and her calls and letters became fewer and further between before ceasing altogether. Aisha must have been embarrassed to have a friend who killed a man, and she would not want the stigma as her legal career took off with civil rights and corruption cases.

So, who was this young man to appear now and undermine her existence? What good would it do anyone dragging up past events? He knew nothing of her world or what she had been through.

If he started telling local people about the shooting, would it make a difference? Some would not believe him, and those that did? Did it matter what they thought?

Rose realised it was inside her that was important and her own sense of right and wrong.

She would continue to protect her family. And although she and Aisha had drifted apart, Aisha had prevented her from languishing in Nanyuki prison, so she would also protect Aisha's children.

She could not change or fully understand the events of forty years ago, but she could bring peace for her old friend, and for her family.

CHAPTER FORTY-THREE

On Thursday morning, Rose returned to the stables at the polo club to check on her patient. The mare had started walking and finally produced a steaming pile of dung, or droppings, which was the horsey term. The syce held up a bucket of water to encourage the horse to drink and he promised to call Rose should the mare have a relapse.

At the clubhouse, Craig had colour in his cheeks for the first time in weeks, and he gave his colleagues a hearty farewell.

"How about stopping in Timau at Mr Isaac's shop?" he suggested. "Now I've met Francis, I'm intrigued to see his father again after so many years. If his shop has remained in the same place, it's near to The Church of the Good Shepherd."

Rose drove steadily up a bumpy track towards the church. She had little choice as pedestrians, bicycles, cows and hens each thought they had the right of way.

They asked directions from a gentleman carrying a sock shop on his person. An array of coloured socks adorned his arms and encircled his neck, yet there appeared not to be a single matching pair.

Rose had always wondered about this and concluded that he only displayed one of each pair, keeping the remaining socks in the large plastic bag he carried. They turned down a narrow side street and pulled up outside a single-storey concrete building, on which a sign announced, "Isaac's Hardware".

"I guess this is the one," said Craig.

"I hope nobody else drives down this street, as there's no room to pass us."

Outside the shop, many items were displayed, including coils of wire, empty plastic vegetable oil containers, crudely carved long wooden handles, and three rolls of vinyl on a metal stand. Inside, the shop was dingy and the small glass counter was covered in dust.

An old-fashioned set of cast iron scales, positioned on the countertop, was evenly balanced with weights and the corresponding amount of half-inch nails. Five sacks of nails of various sizes slumped in the corner. The nails could be bought by the kilo or half kilo and were measured out on the scales and wrapped in a newspaper bundle.

"Can I help you?" A stooped elderly man emerged from the shadows.

"A can of WD 40 please," Craig requested, and enquired, "Mr Isaac?"

"Yes. Should I know you? My sight is failing me, but I recognise your voice."

"Craig Hardie and my wife, Rose. I used to manage Chemchemi Farm."

"Of course, bwana Hardie. Come through. It's too dark in here."

They followed the old man into a second room, which was part store and part workshop.

Several old anglepoise lamps illuminated a wooden workbench on which a piece of wood and various hand tools lay. On a shelf beside it were beautifully carved giraffes, elephants and buffaloes.

Such items were numerous in Nanyuki and were sold to tourists and visiting British Army soldiers, so it was easy to forget the skill involved in sculpting them.

"We recently met your son Francis," Craig told Mr Isaac, who hung his head.

"He's a clever boy, and he worked hard at school. I was so proud when he received a scholarship to Meru University, but now he's a government officer who likes flashy, expensive things. He forgets his roots, his family and his community. They are the important things in life." The old man shook his head of white hair.

"Does he visit you?" asked Rose. She really wanted to ask if Francis helped his father financially, but Mr Isaac, although poor and elderly, was proud and would be offended by such a question.

"Occasionally, but he's too busy meeting or having dinner with important people to bother about me, and I hear he always has a pretty girl on his arm."

CHAPTER FORTY-FOUR

On Thursday afternoon, Rose parked in the yard at the rear of Guinea Fowl Cottage. Francis's Subaru was not there, but the Rav 4 and Land Cruiser were parked under the shade netting. She and Craig had eaten a simple late lunch of baked potatoes, cold ham and salad.

Craig had enjoyed his morning out, particularly his meeting at the Polo Club. Despite the limited mobility of his leg, he had learnt to play polo when he arrived in Kenya as a young man, and he continued playing whenever he had the means and opportunity.

Rose knew that attending the committee meetings helped him feel part of the community again and boosted his self-esteem.

Thabiti walked out of the side door of the house and muttered conspiratorially, "I need to speak to you. Somewhere we can't be overheard." He wrinkled his brow and bit his bottom lip.

"Well, what about my Land Rover?" Rose suggested.

Back in her car, Rose cleared the footwell on the passenger side, and unlocked the door for Thabiti. She noticed he was clutching something in his hand and that his eyes did not meet hers.

"Let me guess, a set of car keys was not the only thing you found on the roof. What's in your hand?"

Thabiti slumped back in his seat and opened a trembling hand.

"It's a pearl earring," said Rose.

"Yes, and I think it's Pearl's pearl earring."

"I see. Have you checked?"

"How? I can't say, 'Hi, I found this earring on the roof of the casino, is it yours?' And I can't start rifling through her things. But what if it is Pearl's? She was upset last night when we returned from the casino. She kept telling me Francis's behaviour wasn't fair, not after what she did for him." Thabiti bit his lip again.

"That doesn't sound great. After Daniel's conduct towards her in Dormans, I doubt he would have met her on the roof out of friendship. But she could have followed him, or someone else, onto the roof," Rose considered.

Thabiti fiddled with the earring and said, "When we met her coming out of the ladies, she appeared agitated and there was a red mark on her arm. What does it mean? What has she done? What has she got herself mixed up in?"

Rose touched Thabiti's arm. "Take a deep breath. All we have is an earring which may or may not be Pearl's, which someone dropped on the casino roof at some point. Don't jump to conclusions. And it's hardly surprising Pearl was agitated considering the way Francis fawned over the President's niece. They may have had a row before we arrived, and that is why she was flustered and had the red mark."

Thabiti sat back in his seat again, closed his eyes and took a deep breath. "Sorry, I was rather worked up. And I've got something else. It dropped into my palm when I handed the caterer's keys to the commissioner." Thabiti reached into his pocket and removed the gold disk.

Rose held it to the light to examine it. "I think this is half of a gold cufflink, as it has several small links of chain on the back. It's rather fine, with this red stone inlay. We should check with the commissioner and see if Daniel was wearing cufflinks. But I had him down as a single cuff button man myself. This could mean another man was on the roof."

Rose tried to hand the gold disc back, but Thabiti shook his head. He handed Rose the earring and said, "Can you keep them. What shall we tell the commissioner?"

Rose replied, "Nothing yet. Craig suggested I follow the money, meaning we should find out where Daniel's new found wealth came from.

Let's see if the commissioner has found out anything about that or Daniel's death. But first, I want us to have a really good search for the murder weapon, as I feel certain it's still at Guinea Fowl Cottage."

CHAPTER FORTY-FIVE

Thabiti, Rose and Doris stood in the moderately sized kitchen of Guinea Fowl Cottage on Thursday afternoon. Along one side stood wall units and a freestanding gas cooker, and on the opposite wall more units and a sink.

At the far end, the door leading to the dhobi room was propped open. "We're looking for an object which is reasonably heavy, probably made of wood or metal, and which could easily be swung to hit a small area at the base of the skull. A saucepan would be too large and a knife too sharp."

She picked up a wooden breadboard from behind the toaster. "The flat side of this is too big." She turned the board over. "But the edge could be used." She made a sharp swinging motion with the board and Doris jumped back, a hand flying to quell a squeal.

"Where have you already looked?" Rose asked.

"I look in all flower beds," responded Doris. "I just find broken glasses, beaded flip flop and some teeth, plastic, not real." Doris looked disappointed, as if she had expected to discover a chest full of old coins.

"I didn't have much more luck in the yard," Thabiti admitted. "Just some broken tools, cracked buckets and pieces of pipe. I wondered about some wooden handles, but they were long, like those used on mops. It would be rather hard to deliver a precise blow."

"I agree, a bit unwieldy."

"I check house when I clean, but I see nothing." Doris shrugged her shoulders.

"No problem, we'll take another look and it'll be easier with the three of us," Rose said. "Doris, can you start in the dhobi room, and we'll begin in the kitchen."

They opened cupboards and searched behind tins of beans, packets of rice and bags of sugar. The drawers under the worktops contained the expected cutlery and kitchen knives, and one was filled with paper receipts.

"No sign of Francis. I take it he didn't sleep here last night," enquired Rose.

"He didn't, but he arrived this morning with that enormous bunch of flowers." Thabiti pointed towards a vase filled with yellow, orange and red roses. "He was full of smiles and apologies, but he was talking to a closed door, literally. Pearl wouldn't see him, and she's been in her room all day. Still, after a few more grovelling apologies and expensive gifts and I expect she'll relent."

"I'm not so sure," said Rose. She opened the oven and peered inside. Nothing. On the worktop was a blue-glazed pot filled with various cooking implements. Rose spotted a rolling pin, which she picked up and examined. She replaced it when she found nothing unusual.

"I find this." Doris rushed into the kitchen, waving a hammer.

Thabiti ducked out of her way. "Careful. We use that hammer for hanging pictures. In Nairobi, many of the houses we've lived in had concrete walls, and it's really hard to knock in nails or picture hooks. That's why we use such a large-headed hammer."

Rose examined it. The flat end could have been used as the murder weapon, but as she swung it, she thought it would leave quite a dent and probably some broken bone. "Good find, Doris, but I don't think this is it."

Was she wasting their time on a wild aardvark chase? They had no idea what the murder weapon was or where it could be. Someone could have carried it away, or thrown it over the fence where it would remain undiscovered for weeks.

They completed their search of the kitchen and dhobi room and moved into the living room. A bleary-eyed Pearl appeared, wrapped in a pink kikoi dressing gown. Rubbing her eyes, she asked, "What are you doing? Looking for something?"

"Yes, sorry if we disturbed you," Rose said in a gentle tone.

"Chai," said Doris, who fluttered back to the kitchen.

Rose caught up with Pearl before she reached the veranda. "Pearl, we're searching for the murder weapon. I think it was left here and has been hidden. We've looked outside, in the kitchen and the dhobi room, so if we don't find it in here, can I look in your room?"

Pearl rubbed her neck. "I suppose so. But I doubt you'll find anything and it's rather a mess. Perhaps Doris can help you and tidy up for me."

After Doris delivered Pearl's tea, Rose took her into Pearl's bedroom, and left Thabiti to complete the search of the dining room. Doris clucked at the state of the room and immediately started clearing clothes from the floor, folding them or tossing them into the washing basket.

Rose looked around. Surely the murder weapon wasn't here, not under all these garments, shoes and magazines. What she really wanted was the opportunity to search for Pearl's earrings.

She walked over to a chest of drawers, on top of which were photographs, trinkets and wooden boxes overflowing with costume jewellery, but there were no pearl earrings. The left-hand drawer contained knickers, and Rose hesitated before plunging her hand under piles of silk and lace. Nothing.

She quickly withdrew her hand and rubbed it on her trousers. Opening the right-hand drawer, she breathed out as she would not have to repeat the exercise, since the drawer contained numerous small jewellery boxes.

The third box she opened contained a single pearl earring. Her stomach clenched as she looked at the small black enamel box. Tucked into the lid was a handwritten note, 'All my love, Ma.' Rose looked over her shoulder, and noting that Doris was busy hanging dresses in the wardrobe, she picked up the case and slipped it into her pocket.

As she was about to close the drawer, her eye caught something that should not be there. She reached into the back, behind various coloured boxes, and pulled out a wooden truncheon-shaped object with a metal end.

She turned round and examined it in the light of a window, which Doris had revealed by drawing back the curtains. What had she found?

"That not ours. It belong to barman," stated Doris, apparently unconcerned by its appearance in Pearl's room.

"What was he using it for?" Rose said as Thabiti walked in, followed by Pixel.

"Found something?" he asked.

"Squashing small mint leaves which he put in jugs," continued Doris.

Pixel searched the bedroom, sniffing in corners, at furniture and sticking her nose under the bed.

Thabiti leaned forward to inspect the object. He reached for his phone whilst Rose continued her examination. The object was about ten inches long and could give someone a nasty blow.

Reading from his phone, Thabiti stated, "It's called a muddler, and used in cocktail making."

"Can you have a look at the end? I think something's caught in it, but I can't see well enough." Rose handed the muddler to Thabiti, who held it up to the window. A small strand hung down, caught between the wood and the metal, which Thabiti extracted.

"A thread of red material." He said, holding it up.

"Could it be from your mother's headscarf?" Rose asked.

"Potentially. So have we found the murder weapon?" Thabiti's brow wrinkled.

"Very possibly, and for the lack of anything else, let's call it Exhibit A. Tomorrow we need to find that elusive barman Sam. And he has some explaining to do regarding this and his appearance, and disappearance, as a doorman at the casino last night."

Thabiti asked, "How are you going to find him?"

"I'll sleep on it. Good work, team. We're making progress, if only very slowly."

Rose looked across at Thabiti and decided not to mention the earrings. Not yet, anyway. "Thabiti, it's been a busy day, but we do need to visit Commissioner Akida."

"Do I have to?" Thabiti mumbled, shuffling his feet.

"Yes, you do. We need to tell him we found the murder weapon, nothing else, and I want to see if he's found out anything connected with Daniel's death."

CHAPTER FORTY-SIX

R ose, with a reluctant Thabiti, found Commissioner Akida in his office at the police station on Thursday afternoon. In the corner, the potted fern had lost its vibrant appearance and looked dishevelled. No doubt a result of the awful tea and coffee the commissioner fed it. The commissioner, who was capless, ran his fingers through his greying hair.

"Bad business, bad business," he repeated, indicating to Rose and Thabiti to sit on the chairs opposite his desk. He picked up his open penknife and a small piece of wood, and continued to carve an unidentifiable shape.

Rose began, "Commissioner, we have some good news. We've found the murder weapon."

The commissioner abruptly stopped his whittling and put down his model. He turned the muddler in his hand as he scrutinised it.

"Why do you think this killed Aisha?" he asked.

"Someone suggested a rolling pin, which this resembles," replied Rose. "A man or woman could wield it and deliver a precise blow, but not one that would shatter the skull."

The commissioner swiped the air. "That seems a reasonable assumption. But why this particular object? What is it?"

"It's called a muddler, and it's used in cocktail making," explained Thabiti. "The barman at Ma's party was using one, possibly this one."

"And we found this piece of thread attached to it. I think it came from Aisha's headscarf," added Rose.

The commissioner turned on his desk lamp to examine the strand. "That is also a logical deduction. Where did you find this muddler?"

Rose responded, "At Guinea Fowl Cottage, although I prefer not to divulge the exact location at the moment."

The commissioner placed the items on his desk, sat back, crossed his arms and frowned at Rose. "That is most irregular. I am a policeman." He resumed his whittling.

"But not in this case. Do you always divulge all the information you gather? I feel as if I'm trying to complete a jigsaw puzzle without all the pieces. I have lots of blue pieces which I think are the sky, but what if they turn out to be the sea?"

The commissioner squeezed his eyebrows together. "I think I understand, but assembling the pieces takes time and could be dangerous. That's why I've decided to take Aisha's case back on Monday, despite the directive from Nairobi, and investigate it alongside Daniel's death."

Rose's stomach clenched. She would lose Aisha's case, and just when she was making actual progress.

The commissioner continued, "I'm sorry. I know you've worked hard, but Daniel's case is complicated, and if it is linked to Aisha's, then neither you nor Thabiti should be anywhere near it."

It was Rose's turn to cross her arms. As she opened her mouth to protest, the commissioner leaned forward. He raised his arm, pointing the penknife at Rose. "I am extremely grateful to you, and I will keep you informed."

Rose sat back, out of range of the knife blade, as the commissioner continued, "In fact, I may need to discuss points with you to get the benefit of your knowledge of the case."

Rose looked towards Thabiti, who gazed at the ceiling. He looked relieved, but that was not surprising since the evidence currently pointed towards his sister.

Rose pursed her lips. She still had Friday and the weekend, but it would now be best to continue her enquires on her own, without Thabiti.

Constable Wachira arrived, interrupting her thoughts. She carried a white plastic bag and looked across at the commissioner, who nodded.

"Habari. I've just returned from Avocado Catering where I was told Daniel had this bag at the casino." She placed the plastic bag on the commissioner's desk. "It contains a bottle of water, a jumper and some spare shoes, none of which are particularly interesting. But I also found this."

From the bag, the young policewoman extracted a folded piece of paper on which was scribbled "Roof 6.25".

"Well, well," mused the commissioner. "This is proof he was meeting someone, and the time fits. To reconfirm, you were in the casino at that time?" He looked across at Rose and Thabiti.

Rose replied, "Yes, we were speaking with the chefs, so it couldn't be either of them."

"What about our barman-cum-casino doorman?" All eyes turned to Constable Wachira, whose cheeks flushed. Avoiding their eyes, she flipped through a notebook and continued, "He was at the door of the VIP suite from six o'clock when the first guests arrived."

"Did he say who they were?" asked Rose.

The constable handed Rose her notebook. "He didn't know everyone's names, so gave me descriptions as well."

Rose looked down the list, hoping her face remained impassive as she saw Pearl and Francis's names jotted down as arriving at five past six. So Pearl had arrived with Francis, and not after him, as she had presumed.

This did not look good for Pearl. "Thank you." She returned the notebook. Everyone looked expectantly at her, so she mumbled, "Interesting."

"Mama Rose, you are rather tight-lipped this afternoon," observed the commissioner. "And I am not sure about sharing the next piece of information with you as it's rather personal." He looked across at Thabiti, closed his penknife and lay it on the desk.

"Why, what have I done?" Thabiti cried.

"Nothing, I hope, but we are confused. Constable Wachira will explain."

Constable Wachira began, "You suspected Daniel had recently come into money because he wore expensive new accessories, so we searched his house and found more items, including some pricey electronic devices. But we didn't find any cash, so I checked his Mpesa statements. He recently received a large sum from 'Aisha Onyango'."

"What? Why was Ma sending him money?" Thabiti threw up his arms.

The young constable answered, "She wasn't, but it appears her phone was. The payment was made on the evening of her death, but later, just after ten o'clock. My guess is someone used her phone. Someone who knew her passwords."

Thabiti shook his head. "Are you accusing me? Both…" He stopped abruptly.

"Were you about to say both Pearl and you knew her passwords?" The commissioner leaned forward.

Thabiti nodded slowly.

"I have to admit, it is not looking good for your sister. Money was sent from a phone she had access to, and she entered the VIP suite at five past six. She had time to send the note and meet Daniel," stated the commissioner.

Rose waited, expecting a verbal outcry from Thabiti, but he looked dejected, slumped in his chair. Did he think Pearl killed Daniel? He had also found the earring on the roof, something they had both failed to tell the commissioner. Rose realised she was treading a very thin line.

"But what motive would Pearl have to harm Daniel?" asked Rose.

The commissioner rested his elbows on his desk and knitted his fingers together, holding her gaze. "The obvious one is that Daniel saw her kill Aisha, blackmailed her, and in turn Pearl killed him."

"But why kill her mother?" asked Rose.

"Money and freedom would be my guess." The commissioner looked grim.

Thabiti was examining his feet.

"Commissioner, Pearl's fallen out with Francis and locked herself in her room today. She isn't going anywhere. If we keep an eye on her, can you wait until Monday to question her?" Rose paused. "I keep visualising sheep."

Opening his arms on his desk, the commissioner repeated, "Sheep!"

"Yes. Someone's pulling the wool over our eyes."

CHAPTER FORTY-SEVEN

O n Friday morning, Rose was seated at the corner table in Dormans coffee shop. The previous evening Chloe, the attractive lady who was new to Nanyuki, had called, demanding all the news from the casino opening night and the man who had fallen from the roof. Rose, too exhausted by the day's events to discuss it, reluctantly agreed to meet this morning for coffee.

She felt a heaviness in her chest. On her last visit, Daniel had been alive, and she'd given him a grilling. What a waste of a life. Had he been blackmailing someone? Pearl perhaps?

"Rose," exclaimed Chloe, intruding on her introspection. "What an exciting place Nanyuki is, after all. I was outside the casino and saw that man fall, but I understand you have the ear of the police, and some inside knowledge. Tell me all about it." Chloe sat down and looked expectantly at Rose.

Rose stared back, and pressed, "You saw him fall? What exactly did you see?"

Chloe sat back. "Well, a man plunging through the air. I looked away before he hit the ground, but it sounded like a large metal garbage bin being slammed shut. I had expected a thump or a splat. You know I've never seen a person die."

Chloe's excitement turned to despondency. She squeezed her eyes shut, slowly shaking her head.

Poor girl has finally realised we're talking about a human life? Rose laid a hand on Chloe's arm.

"Tell me, was he falling forwards or backwards? Feet-first or head-first?" asked Rose, in a quiet but firm tone.

Chloe sniffed. "I hadn't thought about that." She stood up and looked along the street towards the casino building. "He was facing the building, and to start with it looked as if he'd stepped backwards off the roof. Then his back arched, his head came down, and I guess he landed on his back. Why? Do you think someone pushed him?"

"I'm not sure. Did you see anyone else on the roof?"

"Possibly a shadow, but nothing definite." They ordered their drinks from a waitress and then Chloe continued, "I was so excited about the casino opening and my first event in Nanyuki. But we didn't stay long as I couldn't stop thinking about that man. I found out yesterday that he was the waiter from here and we'd given him such a hard time."

She stared down at the table on which their drinks were placed. Chloe had reverted to coffee and sipped a large cappuccino, leaving white frothy bubbles splattered on her lips. Unselfconsciously, she wiped them off.

"I saw someone who looked like you at the casino on Wednesday evening, wearing a billowing kanga skirt," remarked Chloe.

Rose blushed. "It was me, and I had to I borrow the skirt. I suppose you could say I was working undercover for the police." They both smiled. "So you know what kanga material is? Which is not to be confused with 'kanga' the bird, which is a guinea fowl."

"Oh, I didn't know, but I love the brightly printed cloth. It's so versatile." Chloe pulled a bundle from her bag and held up a green and red wrap skirt. "Look, I had this made locally. The tailor commented that the women of Nanyuki would soon be wearing the same coloured skirts."

Chloe confided. "Your friend Aisha had one made, and so did her daughter for her mother's party. I'll have to be careful where I first wear this." She neatly folded the skirt and placed it back in her bag.

Rose was sure Pearl wore a dress to the party. She remembered her asking Francis to fasten the zip.

CHAPTER FORTY-EIGHT

R ose didn't have to find Sam, as the elusive barman found her. She returned home on Friday morning from Dormans to find him and Craig conducting an animated discussion about the upcoming inaugural Giants Club Summit.

"Attendees of the summit will visit Ol Pejeta Conservancy, which has an excellent anti-poaching operation. Because of it, there are over a hundred black, and twenty white, rhinos on the conservancy," remarked Sam.

"But they still have their problems. Why, only last month Ishirini was attacked and killed with poisoned arrows, and her horns were chopped off," responded Craig.

Rose joined in. "I understand she was pregnant and near to full term. It's so appalling that poaching at this level continues."

"Yes, dear," said Craig. "I think you've already met Sam."

Sam stood and offered his hand. Rose took it gingerly, feeling this huge man could snap her in half.

"We haven't been formally introduced. Sam Mwamba, employee of the Kenya Anti-Poaching Unit and colleague of the late Aisha Onyango."

"Well, this rather turns matters on their head." Rose made herself comfortable on the cedar sofa. "Why didn't you tell me before? Do the police know who you are?"

Sam spoke in an easy, relaxed manner with a soft drawl. "My work in the unit is sensitive, and despite my size, or perhaps because of it, I undertake a lot of undercover work."

Sam's jaw was set. "Please understand, anything we discuss today, we need to keep to ourselves.

I'm sure you realise how important infiltrating the poaching rings is, and we need to reach those controlling them at every level. As to why I didn't tell you before, I guess I wasn't sure I could trust you. I've also been tied up with a case which has taken me in and out of Nanyuki."

"But you were at the casino on Wednesday evening?" Rose stated.

"For a time, yes." Sam grinned. "I was not the only one working undercover that night. I also saw Aisha's son pretending to be a waiter."

Rose crossed her legs. "How do you know he was pretending and not a paid employee?"

Sam leaned back. "I've learnt to spot the signs. He wasn't used to wearing a bow tie and kept sticking his finger under his collar. And he hung back and found it virtually impossible to circulate amongst the guests, waiting instead for them to approach him. Plus, I have a source within the Nanyuki police who told me you had both been drafted to gather information about the young waiter's death. You had to mingle with other guests and staff."

Rose paused. "Your source wouldn't happen to be a bright, young and female?"

Sam blushed, his cheeks turning pink, and he looked down at his hands. "I see little escapes you."

"Too true, too true," agreed Craig.

"I think we have quite a lot to discuss, young man," said Rose. Potto curled up next to her, and she stroked his back.

"Where would you like to start?" Sam clasped his hands together.

"How about the murder weapon?" suggested Rose.

"I've no idea. I guess something hard with an edge or round like a piece of metal pipe."

"Or a muddler," suggested Rose, watching Sam's reaction.

"A muddler! Is that a person, Rose?" Craig frowned.

Sam glanced at Craig.

Rose responded, "No, we think it's the murder weapon. I haven't had the chance to tell you yet, but we searched Guinea Fowl Cottage yesterday afternoon. And I found a wooden truncheon-shaped item with a piece of red thread caught on it. A muddler is used by barmen to crush herbs and spices for cocktails."

Sam's eyes registered his understanding. "And I was using just such an item last Saturday when preparing mojito cocktails for the party." He raised a finger to his lips. "At least, I used it to start with, but I thought I had mislaid it as I had to use a knife later on."

"Do you have any idea when you last saw it?" Rose asked.

Sam's brow furrowed. Rose and Craig waited. "After Aisha's son left for the second time, but before he returned. I looked for it once I'd sorted out the ice."

"So it went missing over an hour before the body was found," said Rose.

"Yes, I guess that's right."

"So who had the opportunity?" asked Craig.

"Both Daniel and the maid spoke with me when I was setting up the bar. As I left the veranda, via the garden steps, I heard Pearl and Francis come out of the house. I think they were arguing, but I couldn't hear what they said. Pearl wandered back into the house as I returned, but there was no sign of Francis."

Craig queried, "So when you left the veranda, the muddler was available for anyone to take?"

"Only if they'd known Sam had it in the first place and had seen him use it," answered Rose. "I don't think the murder was pre-meditated, otherwise our killer would have brought their own weapon."

Rose asked Sam, "Why were you acting as a barman for Aisha's party?"

"Protection and surveillance, but I failed at both." Sam lowered his eyes. "The work that Aisha and I do, rather she did, is not always popular. Aisha and her colleagues recently completed a survey highlighting the loss of a third of the government's budget through corruption. But the leadership has denied it, as the President came to office pledging to fight corruption."

"It's endemic and almost impossible to tackle, as Aisha's agency has surely found," commented Craig.

Sam stared at the wall behind Rose. "The Kenyan people seem apathetic and unwilling to support the fight."

"They're scared," said Rose. "The police aren't immune to corruption, so it deters people from coming forward and reporting bribery or suspected fraud. All of us are guilty of paying a little something to a policeman when we're stopped and accused of speeding or other traffic violations. We can't be bothered to argue if the allegations are true or not. It's easier and far less scary than going to court or jail."

"Exactly." Sam crossed his arms. "What you do is at the lower level, but those who commit far larger acts of bribery may also justify their action with a moral argument."

He was right, of course, but where should the line be drawn? It was definitely wrong for those in power to invent non-existent projects and steal the funding.

But what about the girl she'd given money to last week? A teenager carrying her baby daughter on her front. The girl tried to register her daughter's birth, as required by law, so she could become a Kenyan citizen.

She took the correct documents and money for the birth certificate to the District Office, but a clerk refused to register her daughter unless she paid a bribe of five hundred shillings.

She was told the alternative was a penalty for late registration, plus a search fee of hospital records for the birth, and the process could take six months.

The girl looked wretched, so Rose had given her a five hundred shilling note, although she realised that by doing so, she had condoned the act of bribery.

"You're unusually quiet, Rose," interrupted Craig.

"Sorry, I was lost in my own thoughts." Rose focused on Sam. "Getting back to Aisha and her commission's survey…"

Sam said, "A growing area of corruption is the county health departments. Aisha had started investigations into their equipment purchase procedures. She told me some equipment supply companies were alarmed by her probing, and they were using their contacts in central government to put pressure on her."

"Is one of these suppliers Jeremiah Angote?" Rose asked.

"Yes, I believe so," Sam replied. "Do you know him?"

"No, but I've heard about him." Rose remembered the discussion between Francis and Commissioner Akida. "Apparently, the Meru County Health Department is looking to purchase equipment from Mr Angote. And he hosted a dinner that Pearl and Francis attended earlier this week."

Sam frowned. "From what Aisha told me, Jeremiah Angote is a very slippery fish. She was certain someone was trying to intimidate her. There were small things like the feeling of being watched, or being followed in her car, and she thought someone had broken into her house, but nothing had been taken. She believed Jeremiah Angote was behind it. Aisha was one tough lady, but I think the invisible harassment got to her."

Rose asked, "Is that why she moved back to Nanyuki? I didn't think it was because of the trouble Thabiti was having at uni."

"Yes," replied Sam. "That and a new case she was working on which she didn't even tell me about. I suspect it involved hospital equipment and from what you've told me, I'd wager it concerned Meru County Government."

CHAPTER FORTY-NINE

Rose sat on her covered patio on Friday morning with Craig and the large barman, Sam, who actually worked for the Kenya Anti-Poaching Unit and had been a colleague of the late Aisha Onyango.

"On the subject of moving house and break-ins, I have a confession," admitted Sam, rubbing his nose.

"Oh, yes?" enquired Rose.

"I heard from my police source that you believe someone searched Aisha's guest cottage."

Rose wrinkled her brow, and murmured, "Go on."

Sam looked down at his hands and admitted, "I only went there to clear out sensitive papers and files. And I fully expected the maid or gardener to catch me, as the guinea fowl made an indignant outcry. They're quite the guard dogs. I was also looking for Aisha's laptop, but I understand Thabiti took it. Do you know if he has accessed any files?"

Rose shook her head. "Not that I know of, and he's rather frustrated by it."

"I am relieved." Sam leaned back. "That laptop contains information that could put him in danger. It's why Aisha installed such sophisticated US software and shows just how worried she was. Do you think you could persuade him to hand it over to me? Or alternatively, I could ask someone at the Anti-Corruption Commission to collect it. Someone I trust, as we don't want the computer landing in the wrong hands. Sorry, but this job has made me paranoid and I trust very few people."

Rose thought Sam led an interesting but dangerous life. Few people were prepared to put themselves at such risk for the good of their country.

Sam clasped his hands together. "I am sorry I caused Aisha's family more pain and worry. And I should have confided in you earlier."

"What will you do with the laptop if you get it? And what were the papers you took?" Rose asked.

"I hope one of Aisha's colleagues will continue her work, as long as they're not been put off by her death. And if they don't, I might have to call upon you to help, Rose." Sam raised a hand as Craig opened his mouth, presumably to protest. "I jest, although I think you would do a better job than most people. You appear to have a strong moral compass."

Sam sat up in the large cedar chair and rested his hands on its arms. "Investigating corruption is one thing. But resisting the temptation to take bribes yourself is quite another. Most people are unable to refuse the offer of a new house, education for their children or their family's medical worries taken care of."

Sam paused and asked, "Would it be possible to have a cup of coffee and take a short break? What I have to say next is harder to explain."

Craig remained seated, but picked up his latest crossword puzzle. Rose stood, stretched, and walked into the house to ask Kipto for fresh drinks. When she returned, she watched Sam strolling lazily around the garden.

He stopped every few strides to gaze upon Mount Kenya. A blanket of heavy cloud was beginning to encroach on the morning's sunshine. Five minutes later, the group reconvened on the patio with fresh tea and coffee.

Sam began. "Some papers I took from the cottage were not connected to Aisha's professional work, but to a private case she'd asked for my help with. In preparing for her move to Nanyuki, she sorted through her father's possessions and, amongst them, she found numerous newspaper clippings.

"Many were yellowed with age, but the majority had hand-written notes and comments attached to them. Also, there were photographs, reports and documents. Mr Onyango was particularly obsessed with corruption, especially in government, and I understand he was a colleague of Josiah Kariuki, who was assassinated. Josiah believed corruption was the primary cause for the widening gap between rich and poor in the late 1960s and early 1970s."

Craig put down his crossword, but Rose was completely absorbed by Sam's words and her hands trembled.

Sam continued, "There were many documents about poaching. Mr Onyango's interest seems to have begun when Aisha defended you against the alleged shooting and killing of a poacher."

"Alleged?" questioned Rose. "I don't understand. I fired Craig's shotgun and killed a man."

"That's what everyone believed at the time. But have you ever wondered why the case didn't reach court and the charges against you were dropped?"

"I presumed Aisha argued that the men were trespassing, that poaching was illegal, and I was acting in self-defence."

Sam leaned forward in his chair. "If that had been the argument, you could still have been convicted and served a prison sentence. The law on self-defence was uncertain forty years ago. It still is, to some extent."

Rose felt a chill and the weight of Sam's words pressed against her chest. Just where was this leading? Could the case be legally reopened even after all this time?

Sam continued, "When Aisha heard you'd been arrested for murder, her father accompanied her to Rumuruti police station."

Rose felt giddy. "So I didn't imagine Mr Onyango arguing with a senior police officer."

Sam shook his head. "Mr Onyango received kidnap threats against Aisha when she was staying with you. He told the Chief of Police about them but he dismissed the claims."

Rose exclaimed, "So that's why Aisha returned to Nairobi. As the answers to the case were there."

"Aisha and her father worked tirelessly after their return. Mr Onyango redeemed many political favours, and they discovered possible links between government officials, emerging organised criminal groups and poachers."

Sam paused for another drink of coffee, but Rose's eyes remained fixed on him.

Sam set down his coffee cup and said, "To ensure your freedom, Mr Onyango applied pressure to several government officials. One of them finally caved in and agreed to call Rumuruti police station and authorise your release."

The weight on Rose's chest lightened, but she still felt a chill and a tingling sensation. She thought she understood the meaning of Sam's words. That the whole incident had been planned. She looked over at Craig to see if he had put the same pieces of the puzzle together.

Craig opened his mouth, but no sound emerged. He tried again. "Are you saying that the whole event was nothing to do with poaching but an attempt to kidnap Aisha? If so, they were probably watching the house and waiting for me to leave. Oh, Rose, if you hadn't fired at them, you'd probably all be dead. You and the maid, because you were witnesses, and I doubt Aisha would have been returned safely to her father, even if he had complied with their demands."

Rose shuddered, feeling several ghosts walk across her grave.

CHAPTER FIFTY

Rose, Sam and Craig continued their discussion of the events that had happened forty years before at Ol Kilima.

Sam reported, "After Mr Onyango died, Aisha found the kidnap letter and reports, witness accounts and information her father continued to collect. He believed the officials he'd put pressure on were the weaker members of the herd, but he died without discovering the identity of the leaders, or confirming their links with organised crime and poaching."

Craig scratched his chin. "So were they poachers?"

Sam rocked his head and scrunched his lips. "Some were, but Aisha wanted to know more. She was seeking to prove that there continues to be a link between certain officials, members of government and poaching."

Sam paused before continuing. "I agreed to help her and recently visited Ol Kilima."

Rose clasped her hands to her chest.

"Is the old farmhouse a tourist lodge?" asked Craig conversationally.

"It is, but Aisha's father obtained a sketch of the layout of the house and yard as they were when you lived there. Most of the outbuildings have been taken down and rebuilt at the new farm compound. The wall is there, though, and sections were rebuilt where buildings once stood. I was able to put together the gang's likely actions, especially since they thought you'd be unable to defend yourselves."

Sam returned his attention to Rose. "Every account I have is that the group entered the compound together through the yard gate directly behind the house and none of them came through the front garden. Now blood was found on the wall in the yard, but it would have been impossible for you to shoot someone standing there. The kitchen window, through which you fired, was located on the side wall and the range of fire was the garden at the side of the house, through to the back right-hand corner of the yard."

Rose didn't want to remember, to recall those events, but she willed herself to walk through the process of searching for Craig's gun. He'd kept it in his study next to the kitchen and she'd found it in a cupboard.

The shouts and jeers of the men were growing louder, so she'd loaded the gun in the study and run, no, walked back to the kitchen.

The cries were even louder there. The blue gingham curtains flapped above the sink, and the window was open a few inches at the bottom.

She pointed the barrel of the gun through the window and swivelled it towards the back of the house, but she was stopped by a down-pipe. She took aim and fired.

"I couldn't point the gun into the yard, as a drainpipe was in the way, so I fired at the feed room wall. The feed room was the closest building to the house. I didn't see anyone and think I must have been scared and screwed my eyes shut. At least that's what I told the police, but it wasn't true. I remember now, my eyes were open, and I actually aimed at an area below the ring where I tied the horses." Her lungs expanded, and she felt weightless.

Craig said in a faraway voice, "When I returned from Rumuruti, the yard was empty and there was no dead body. I found you girls hiding in the kitchen pantry."

Sam revealed, "The police records state that the body was brought to the police post at Ol Kilima village the following day. The man had been shot in the leg and died from his wounds, which I take to mean he bled to death. Of course, there was no autopsy and no further record of his injuries. However, I was directed to a nearby village and an old mzee, who had been a constable at the police post and took delivery of the body. There's no love lost between him and poachers, as he was subsequently shot in the arm by one."

Sam drained the remains of his coffee. "First, he confirmed the body was that of the man named in the incident report. A local man called Kafara who'd recently married and whose wife was expecting their first child. One of those who brought the body was a local teenager. At the time, the old policeman thought the boy was ill as he was sweating and he vomited when the body was produced. But looking back, he wondered if the boy had been beaten. Three older men accompanied him, and they weren't locals. There was a hardness about them and one displayed several gold rings."

Kipto bustled onto the patio and cleared away the tea and coffee cups. Rose's cup was still full of cold brown tea. Sam waited before continuing.

"The body was covered in dirt and blood. A crude bandage, made from a strip of material, had been wrapped around the upper thigh and was caked in blood. When the policeman tried to remove the bandage, the men stopped him. Their cries woke the sergeant, who came out to see what the fuss was. He wandered off with one of the hard-looking men, telling the policeman to guard, but not touch, the body. And when the sergeant returned, he sent the policeman to fetch the priest and the dead man's family."

"For a hasty burial, no doubt," interjected Craig.

"Yes, when the policeman returned, the body had been loaded onto a handcart and covered, so that only the face was visible. The burial took place immediately, and one of the men thrust a bunch of notes into the hands of the grieving widow."

Payment for her husband's services, or her silence, wondered Rose.

"The policeman told me the image of the bandage never left him, and as he dealt with more gunshot wounds during his career, he gradually worked out what was wrong. An entry wound from a shotgun cartridge is messy, but the bullet of a rifle has a clean entry, with the damage being done on exiting the body. In this case, the larger hole was at the back of the thigh."

"I'm falling behind. Why is that relevant?" asked Rose.

"The hole in the back of the thigh means you would have to had shot him as he moved away from the house, and at relatively close range. But there are no accounts this happened. The records state that he was shot in the rear yard whilst moving towards the house. Are you with me so far?" Sam asked.

Craig and Rose nodded in unison.

"But if a rifle had been used, it would have made this type of wound with the victim facing his killer. By the mid-1970s AK47s were available in Kenya and it's my guess this is the weapon which actually killed Mr Kafara."

"Then Rose didn't kill him," said Craig in a hushed tone.

Rose felt even lighter and tears began to fall, silently at first, and then in large sobs.

"It looks that way." Sam lifted his arms, then let them fall. "The records show Rose was not arrested until a week later, by which time the teenage boy who had been a witness had also vanished. I think Rose was just another victim." He looked across at Rose, "And conveniently, you never denied firing the shotgun."

Rose's arms fell limply to her side. "I didn't see any point. The maid and Aisha saw me. I'd only hit a wall so I couldn't see any harm admitting it."

"Right until the point you ended up in Rumuruti jail." Sam smiled sadly.

"Yes." Rose felt ice return to her body. "I felt so lonely and helpless. Over and over again, the policemen shouted at me for shooting a young man. They assured me they had witnesses who'd testify against me."

Rose remembered the wobbly wooden table with the green-painted legs. The end of one leg had snapped off, and the table bucked every time one of the policemen shifted his weight. The sight fascinated Rose as the accusations and insults had rained down on her.

"In the end I was so exhausted I think I just agreed with them. Anything for some fresh air, water and a piece of bread."

CHAPTER FIFTY-ONE

Rose sat on the cedar sofa on her outdoor patio, struggling to understand all the information Sam had given her about the events that happened forty years before, at Ol Kilima.

The poachers had not been poachers, but men hired to abduct Aisha. The dead man had not been shot by her shotgun but by an AK47, although that couldn't be proven.

Craig had not let her down, but had been another victim as the gang had waited for him to leave. Aisha had not been angry with her, but had been protecting her. All she had believed, had lived with for forty years, was an illusion created to conceal more malevolent actions.

"All that's missing is evidence," Rose sighed. "We can't prove any of this."

Sam nodded. "But I have one final lead to pursue and I'm leaving for Nairobi after this meeting. One of my less law-abiding contacts has located a man who was part of the gang who entered your compound. He lives in Mombasa now, but he will be in Nairobi tomorrow, and he's reluctantly agreed to meet with me."

"Will he sign a confession or a witness statement?" asked Craig.

Sam stiffened and replied, "Certainly not, and he'll deny everything he tells me. I shall write down an account of our conversation and it'll be on record as hearsay, but it will have no legal standing. But his confession should be sufficient to clear you, perhaps not in law, but morally, and in the eyes of God."

"But what about Mr Kafara's grandson, if that's who he is?" asked Rose.

"Oh, he's the grandson, all right. Has he been bothering you?" Sam's lip curled. "The lazy piece of garbage. His father died, leaving him in charge of his mother, grandmother and two school-age sisters, but he shirks his responsibilities. The entire family work on their small shamba growing vegetables to feed themselves, and while his mother mends clothes to make a few shillings, he goes off drinking."

"I thought as much," said Craig, puffing his chest out.

"When he heard I was asking about his grandfather, he started following me around, and tried to get me to tell him what had happened, and who might be to blame."

Rose sat on her hands. "Clearly he still suspects I am, as he's been here threatening us and demanding money."

"Waster," spat Sam. "I suspect he chatted up the old policeman who inadvertently revealed where you lived."

"And he's coming back tomorrow to collect a hundred thousand shillings, but we don't have that much money, here or in the bank." Rose rocked on her hands.

Sam looked from Rose to Craig and said, "If you'd like me to sort him out, I could stay in Nanyuki, and be here tomorrow to confront him."

Rose looked at him wide eyed. "But what about your meeting?"

"Well, the gentleman's due to return to Mombasa, so it might be the only chance I get to speak with him."

"No, you mustn't cancel. You must see if he can clear up what happened back then, at Ol Kalima."

Rose looked at Craig, who declared, "We'll manage tomorrow… somehow."

CHAPTER FIFTY-TWO

Rose woke on Saturday morning feeling tired and fuzzy-headed. She was worried about Craig, who'd moaned in pain like a wounded animal during the night. As she padded to the bathroom, early morning light filtered through the flimsy curtains. On her return, she found Craig struggling to sit up.

She rushed to his side. "Let me help." She re-arranged his pillows and part pulled, part lifted him into a sitting position, before slumping on the edge of the bed.

They were both panting. Potto yawned and resumed his sleeping position at the bottom of the bed.

Craig placed a hand on Rose's pale, exposed thigh. "Sorry old girl, I'm becoming a bit of a burden." He smiled feebly and Rose felt as if his hand squeezed her heart and not her leg.

She looked away. "I'll fetch your medicine."

Rose returned with a glass of water, Craig's painkillers and a brave face. She asked, "You're not going to get better, are you?" She bit her bottom lip.

Craig's eyes were clear and steady as he replied, "No, the road ahead is short, but I've enjoyed a grand life."

Rose's chest ached as she watched Craig. She knew he was being stoic for her sake, but that he realised she understood the implications.

Rose crossed to the window, opened it and gazed out on the shadowy garden and the mountain awaking from its slumber.

They'd met at Nakuru Sports Club in 1970 when Craig arrived from Scotland to work in a local accountancy firm. She had perfected an outward persona as a strong, independent young woman, but inside she was lonely, a condition which today would have been diagnosed as depression.

She had dismissed Craig, who even then walked with a limp and came across as a quiet, dour Scotsman. But Craig was patient and maintained a kind and even manner with her.

He was clear-headed and as her loneliness receded, she started to rely on his mental and emotional strength. They were married in 1975, forty-one years ago. A lifetime.

She turned back to Craig and smiled. He smiled back.

She handed him her iPad, together with his glasses, so he could he read the day's news while she changed and prepared for the day ahead.

Kipto poked her head round the door and asked, "Tea?"

Rose looked back at Craig and he nodded, understanding that she was asking if he wanted help to get dressed. This would be the third time she and Kipto had needed to help him. He lifted the duvet and tried to move his legs across the bed.

"Kipto," she called. The housemaid's head reappeared. "First, we must help bwana Craig."

The two women peeled off Craig's pyjamas and pulled on his clothes. The process was unemotional. Kipto had shown no embarrassment the first time they dressed Craig and now Rose thought Craig had lost his own inhibitions, although he was still despondent about needing their help.

Their early morning routine complete, Rose and Craig sat outside on the covered patio, enjoying their first cups of tea.

Kipto placed Craig's bowl of porridge in front of him and put his toast, covered by a frayed tea towel, nearby. She looked at Rose and declared, "Market?"

CHAPTER FIFTY-THREE

On Saturday mornings, Nanyuki holds its second fruit and vegetable market of the week, the first being on a Wednesday.

Rose drove a grumbling Kipto slowly through a crowd of women, most of whom had completed their shopping and were carrying plastic bags, or reed baskets, brimming with produce.

Rose wondered how the driver of a boda-boda would stay upright as two plump ladies loaded themselves, and several bags of vegetables, onto his motorbike.

Kipto tutted. "These ladies buy best quality fruit and vegetables. I have to pick pieces that are not too small or rotten."

All the parking spaces by the entrance to the market were occupied, so Rose stopped to let Kipto out and then drove round to the rear.

She parked on an area of rutted ground beside several wooden stalls selling curtains. She occasionally bought from them, but more often than not, they only had a single curtain.

A pair might leave Europe, but the bales of clothes, curtains and bedding were separated and repacked several times before arriving in Nanyuki and many other towns across Kenya. Sometimes the matching curtain arrived several weeks later.

As she got out of her car, two ragged and dirty children approached her cautiously. They were a boy and girl of around six or seven years old, who walked across the rough-baked ground barefooted. They did not say or do anything except look at Rose with enormous round eyes.

Rose's heart melted. There was still such poverty, with far too many people attempting to survive without adequate food, shelter or clothing.

Rose remembered a jam sandwich she had made as part of her breakfast, but had forgotten to eat on the way to market. She opened the car door, found the plastic bag, and removed the sandwich. She handed one piece to each child, expecting them to break out in squeals of joy and stuff it into their mouths. But instead, they chorused, "Asante Mama," and waited.

A crowd of similarly clad children picked their way towards them and without making a sound, the jam sandwich was torn into minuscule pieces and shared between every child. It reminded Rose of the gospels in the Bible, which reported Jesus feeding five thousand people with just two fishes and five loaves of bread. Only when everyone had a piece did the children eat.

The temporary second-hand clothing, or mitumba, stalls were still setting up on low wooden tables. Some vendors tipped out bags, creating haphazard piles while others carefully folded and laid out their clothes. Whilst she waited, Rose wandered up an alley of potato and carrot sellers in the vegetable market.

Some vendors filled recycled white or yellow buckets with vegetables, but experienced buyers picked pieces from the mounds of carrots or potatoes piled on tarpaulins. All too often, inferior vegetables were hidden at the bottom of the buckets.

She took her time, and when she reached a crossroads, she pondered her next move. She spotted Kipto waving her arms at another lady who looked like Doris, but they were too far away for Rose to see clearly.

The second woman appeared to notice Rose, and as both women turned in her direction, Kipto beckoned with her hand. She grabbed her companion's arm and walked towards Rose. It was Doris, but why was she trying to escape Kipto's grasp?

"What's going on?" Rose asked.

"Doris is scared," replied Kipto.

"Of whom? Me, or you grabbing her arm?"

With a guilty smile, Kipto let go of the squirming Doris as Rose placed a conciliatory hand on her arm and said, "It's OK. You don't need to be scared of me."

"Miss Pearl is who scare me. She appear quiet like mouse, but she have sharp claws, and now her young man have eye for another."

So they've still not made up, Rose thought. "Is there something you want to tell me? About Pearl and Francis?"

Doris looked at the ground and shuffled her feet. "I know it wrong to tell no one what I see. I tell Kipto today and she say I tell you." She paused and took a deep breath.

"On the morning she die, the mistress join Miss Pearl and her man. She drink coffee, but they up late and eat breakfast. Thabiti come back with paper and leave on table when he go again."

"The mistress read paper and she angry, ask Mr Francis things. Who is this man? I not remember name. Are you involved with this? Then she say, you can't be trusted, greedy, self-centred. She roll up newspaper and wave in Francis face. I remember. 'This is my case now and none of you will get away with it. Now leave. Get out of my house. I don't want you seeing Pearl anymore.'

I overhear this from door to veranda." She stopped, gulping in breaths of air and looked at Rose.

"Is there more?"

Doris bit her lip. "Miss Pearl get cross, say nasty things to the mistress. I not say again. She say she go too. Not like the mistress tell her what to do, who to see. The mistress laugh, tell her she not like live on own, she need money, like pretty things. Then she say 'how long will that ambitious young man stay with a penniless girl like you? He only wants my contacts.' Mr Francis not go. He and Miss Pearl stay in bedroom all day."

"Doris, why didn't you tell me this before?"

"Miss Pearl see me. Tell me I not keep job if tell other person. Say she tell everyone I am thief. Then I no get work. I got family, I need job."

Kipto borrowed a yellow vegetable bucket from a stall, and turned it upside down for Doris to sit on. After telling them all she had overheard on the morning of Aisha's death, Doris had started to tremble and shake.

Rose gave her a bottle of water. She always carried water in her mitumba shopping basket as she found searching through the array of clothes hot, thirsty work.

"Asante, Mama Rose. I good now." Doris prepared to stand up.

"One minute, Doris. There's something else I meant to ask you. It's about a kanga skirt. Apparently both Pearl and Aisha had similar coloured kanga skirts made by a tailor in Nanyuki, which they were to wear at Aisha's party."

Doris inclined her head, concentrating hard as Rose continued, "I only saw Pearl wearing a dress, but I remember you mentioned ironing a skirt for her."

Doris nodded enthusiastically. "I did and I see her wear it. She come to kitchen when I wash up. I find skirt on bedroom floor, roll up in ball, when I go in with you, Mama."

"Can you remember what time you saw Pearl in the kitchen?" asked Rose.

"Er... I wash chopping boards and knives, so chefs finish main food. They make puddings."

"Quite late then."

"Yes. Soon after I see her, Daniel shout mistress is dead." Doris' hand flew up to her mouth. She unscrewed the water bottle with shaking hands and took another slug. Some water escaped down her chin and dripped onto the floor.

"Pole," she stammered.

Rose shook her head. "It doesn't matter, but thank you for telling me all this."

Rose walked away, leaving Kipto comforting Doris, whose head was bowed as her shoulders shook.

She left the vegetable stalls for the turmoil of the mitumba market. Several men and women stood on their wooden tables shouting about their wares.

Some stallholders sold nearly every type of clothing, while others specialised in trousers or T-shirts, underwear, or items made from fleece. Rose headed to a stall selling women's blouses and tops.

CHAPTER FIFTY-FOUR

The poacher's grandson did not appear until half-way through Saturday afternoon. Rose had lingered at the market and mitumba, half-hoping he would turn up while she was away.

When, after lunch, he had still not arrived, she had become agitated and restless. She had seen and heard many things over the past few days and needed time for everything to settle in her mind.

Kipto announced, "That man back. The one with small eyes, and I think he drink too much. He shout at me to open gate and wave his hands."

"Oh, dear." Rose's shoulders slumped.

"Better let him in, Kipto. And get it over with." Craig attempted to sit up in his cedar chair, but he was still weak.

The young man sauntered around the house and seated himself on the spare chair without being invited. "What a homely afternoon scene," he slurred.

"You've been drinking," declared Craig.

"I had a couple. I'm not used to money in my pocket."

"I bet it's empty now," quipped Rose.

"Perhaps, but you good people are about to refill it for me." The young man sneered.

Rose considered him. Although he appeared confident, the way he tapped his leg and fidgeted in his seat revealed his insecurity. What else was he concealing?

"What do you see when you look at us?" she asked.

"A couple of comfortable mzungus who haven't been made to pay for a crime they committed, and can now afford to help a struggling African man."

She leaned towards him, and revealed, "Initially, I saw a young man seeking recompense for the wrongs done to his family. But both appearances are false. The truth lies much deeper. You have no intention of helping your family. If you had, you could have assisted them on the shamba or found paid work. But instead you threaten us in order to get money to feed your own lifestyle and drinking habit."

Rose's cheeks flushed as years of guilt, of believing she was hiding her true self behind a mask of respectability, broke free.

"Your grandfather, he may have been a poacher, but he was also a man for hire, and he was paid to abduct a young woman." The grandson frowned.

"His associates killed him, not me. I have nothing to atone for, so you'll get nothing from me. We are just two old people trying to live out our old age as best we can."

Craig said in a concerned tone, "Rose, steady on. What about the man Sam is meeting today?"

Rose didn't need anyone to confirm the events of that night. She could remember them clearly now, and she knew she hadn't shot anyone. After firing the gun, she had seen two figures emerge from behind the barn and run down the track.

The other men shouted at them with their voices full of hate and cruelty. These men were the reason she'd rushed back to her hiding place, as they'd really scared her.

"There's no proof of what you say. And the records still show you were the one arrested." The young man's defiant voice waived as he finished his statement.

Rose held her head high. "And I was acquitted. But I'll find you evidence if you come back next week. It might not stand up in court, but it'll be good enough to show anyone who doubts my word."

Rose crossed her fingers. Perhaps she was going too far, but she continued, "Go. You're not getting any more money from us."

The grandson frowned and crossed his arms. "You can't get rid of me that easily."

"Someone need getting rid of?" Rose hadn't noticed Pixel scamper around the corner, although Izzy was standing on the sofa with her legs extended and her hair bristling. Thabiti stood behind Craig's chair, leaning forward and staring at the grandson who was now upright, but swaying.

"I'm not going anywhere until I'm paid what I'm owed."

Thabiti took two paces forward, grabbed the grandson's arm, and swung it behind his back. "You were asked to leave politely. This is the not so polite way." Thabiti left, marching the grandson in front of him.

When Thabiti returned, his legs began to shake and so did his voice. "Is there a spare beer?"

This was a side of Thabiti that Rose had not seen. She closed her gaping mouth. "Yes, of course. And you, Craig?"

"Definitely, after that performance."

CHAPTER FIFTY-FIVE

O n Saturday afternoon, Rose, Craig and
Thabiti sat in silence on the covered patio
overlooking Rose's front garden after the
poacher's grandson had left. Craig sipped his
Tusker beer from a glass, while Thabiti slugged
his directly from the bottle.

Rose had a small glass of wine, which she told
herself was to steady her nerves. Even Pixel, Izzy
and Potto were quietly composed next to their
owners.

Thabiti broke the silence. "Mama Rose, I received
your message this morning. So I've looked
through last Saturday's *Standard* newspaper

online. You know, it's amazing how many stories involving corruption are in one edition, but there was only one article relevant to us, or at least to Francis. I had no idea there'd been a row between him and Ma. And all because I took pity on the newspaperman at the road junction and bought a *Standard* from him."

Thabiti opened his laptop.

"Do you need the Wi-Fi code?" Craig asked.

"Don't worry, I've hot-spotted with my phone. Here we are." He carried the computer across to Rose.

"Can you pass my glasses? They're on the dining table." With her glasses perched on her nose, Rose read the piece out loud for the benefit of Thabiti and Craig.

The article centred around the Modern Healthcare Group, which comprised several companies providing healthcare services, medicines and medical equipment. The managing director of MHG was Mr Jeremiah Angote, and he was taking the healthcare sector by storm.

The journalist claimed that his companies were behind five of the leading hospitals in Nairobi, as well as many diagnostic clinics, medical centres and pharmacies.

Following the formation of county governments, the group was expanding its operations, and was engaged in contracts to upgrade outdated medical equipment, as well as providing healthcare services.

However, the journalist alleged that some of the clinics and hospitals receiving the new equipment did not exist, and those that did were paying inflated prices.

The article further claimed that local officials were receiving financial kickbacks in return for placing contracts with MHG. Others were simply pocketing money for facilities that didn't exist. A lengthy list of counties were named in the article, including Meru and the Timau Ward.

"At least Timau Hospital exists," commented Rose.

Thabiti lifted Pixel onto the cedar sofa beside him.

"If Francis works in the Department of Health Services, his remit will be far wider than just Timau. He could be responsible for purchasing equipment or medicine for the entire county, with a budget of several million shillings," noted Craig.

"Francis told us he was hoping to do business with Mr Angote," reflected Rose.

Thabiti stroked Pixel's head. "That could be where he's getting his cash from. And if it is, he wouldn't relish any investigation by the Ethics and Anti-Corruption Committee."

Rose nodded. "Nor would Mr Angote, who has far more to lose. Sam said Aisha was worried about harassment in Nairobi, but this group of companies is countrywide, so they could easily have caused trouble for her in Nanyuki."

"Do you mean Sam, as in the barman? Where did you find him?" Thabiti asked.

Rose laughed. "Oh, he found us. It turns out he was working with your mother. And he knows about all sorts of shady goings on."

Thabiti closed his laptop. "So he's off the hook for the murder?"

"Unless he's an exceptional actor, and has fed us a very convincing story. I can't see what he would gain and he has lost a respected colleague."

Rose leaned towards Thabiti. "Thank you for finding this. Yesterday, the evidence pointed at Pearl, so I hadn't wanted to involve you further. But now I think I need your help, even if Pearl is involved. I feel a lurking menace out there."

Thabiti downed the last of his beer and looked from Rose to Craig. "I also need your help. It's a week since Ma's death, and the time has come to lay her to rest. I would like to arrange the cremation for Wednesday morning. Does that sound reasonable?"

Craig replied, "Reasonable for who, dear boy? She was your mother, but for my part, I think that sounds sensible. Who would you like to invite?"

"You and Rose. And maybe Sam, if he's around and was a close colleague of Ma's. And perhaps the commissioner. There will be Pearl and myself. I don't want Francis there, but Pearl may insist."

"A small group, but I presume you will organise a memorial service?" asked Craig.

"In Nairobi, yes, but I'll need some help. It'll have to wait, though, until things are sorted here."

Rose and Craig nodded.

"The thing is, I want to go to the funeral home to arrange the cremation, but I don't want to go on my own." Thabiti looked down at the floor.

"I'm not very mobile today," said Craig as he turned to Rose. "Can you go with him?"

"Of course." Rose wanted to pay her respects, but she also wanted to see the body again, which she realised was rather morbid.

CHAPTER FIFTY-SIX

Rose and Thabiti arrived at the Community Hospital mortuary at half-past three on Saturday afternoon. It was a single-storey concrete building with yellow-painted walls and a red tin roof, set aside from the other hospital buildings.

A grieving family sat on a bench built around the base of a flame tree.

Thabiti hit the stainless steel reception bell and, despite the sombre atmosphere, grinned like a child. "I always wanted to do that in shops, but Ma wouldn't let me."

A stocky middle-aged woman in blue scrubs waddled in, and with an expressionless face, stated, "Name?"

"Thabiti Onyango." The mortuary assistant looked at him wearily. "Here about my mother, Aisha Onyango."

"Would you like to see her?"

"Er, would we?" Thabiti turned to Rose.

"Yes, we would," Rose directed her response to the lady. She noted that Thabiti was biting his lip.

"Ten minutes. Wait here until I call you."

The waiting room was hot and airless, so Rose wandered outside. The grass had perished, leaving bare baked earth.

Three women sitting on the nearby bench wailed and rocked as they tried to comfort each other. Who had they lost? Was it someone who had lived a long, perhaps hard, life? Or was it a child, snatched from its parents before it had a chance to explore the world?

Rose spotted a young boy sitting on the dirt, marking circles with a broken stick. Why was it that children appeared more resilient than adults when it came to death, but who knew what the long-term effects were, particularly if they lost a sibling.

"Mama Rose, she's ready for us," Thabiti called from the mortuary doorway.

They entered a small room dominated by a stainless steel gurney on which, Rose presumed, was Aisha's body, covered by a dirty yellow sheet.

"Ready?" The mortuary assistant whipped back the sheet without waiting for a response.

Rose had expected Thabiti to turn away or even leave the room, but instead he stepped forward. The bruising around Aisha's eyes had either dissipated or been covered by makeup.

"She looks so peaceful." Thabiti reached out to touch the body and then snatched his hand back and shivered. "But so cold!"

Rose swallowed, and tried to clear her mind and forget that her dead friend lay before her. She felt the body still had something to tell her.

"Doris was right. She did put up a fight. Her fist is still clenched," noted Thabiti. He moved around the table and cried, "She's clutching something."

Rose joined him and saw the tip of a feather protruding from Aisha's closed fist. She looked at the mortuary assistant and asked, "Is it possible to see what she's holding?"

The assistant responded curtly, "Have you finished viewing the body?" Rose and Thabiti looked at Aisha's body, then at each other and nodded. "Then wait outside while I try to open her hand."

After a few minutes, the assistant reappeared, carrying a silver clip with crumpled guinea fowl feathers.

"It looks like a brooch," said Rose.

Thabiti whispered, "No, that's Pearl's hair braid clip. And I think she was wearing it on Saturday."

Rose walked outside, examining the clip as she thought. Thabiti remained in the mortuary, having told Rose he felt able to discuss the arrangements for the cremation directly with the mortuary assistant. He reappeared scratching his head and holding a sheet of paper.

"My invoice. Dying is expensive."

CHAPTER FIFTY-SEVEN

Rose arrived early at Christ the King Catholic Church on Sunday morning. Her sleep the previous night had been deep and apparently dreamless, but little snippets of evidence niggled at the edge of her mind.

It wasn't that she expected a divine revelation whilst she sat quietly on her wooden pew with her head bent, but rather that the peace and solace of God's house would crystallise her thoughts. She was sure she'd collected most of the details of Aisha's case, but she could not grasp the answer.

Her first suspect had been Daniel, whose motive was his grudge against the Onyango family, and he'd had the best opportunity, being back and forth between the house and the outside tent.

And the means? It was clear anyone at the house could have removed the muddler from the bar on the veranda, including Daniel. But did the use of a muddler, rather than a weapon brought specifically to kill Aisha, mean it was an opportunistic murder rather than a premeditated one?

The two chefs told her that Daniel had tried to avoid working the day of the murder, so either he hadn't planned to kill Aisha, or he'd had cold feet about doing so. And what about the money? If someone paid Daniel to kill Aisha, then a second person was involved.

Daniel had received money and spent it on expensive items. The commissioner thought Daniel was blackmailing the actual killer which was consistent with Daniel's character. He had appeared sly and was unlikely to care about justice and report a crime, when he could gain personally from it.

Then there was the Mpesa payment, the money sent via Aisha's phone. Rose didn't know the exact amount, nor did she know if it was the only payment Daniel received.

The identity of the person who sent the Mpesa was unknown, but Pearl was top of the list as she had access to the phone and knew the passwords. Either that or Thabiti had been deceiving her this past week and was involved in his mother's death. It looked like Daniel had been involved and either received money to either commit the murder, or keep quiet about it.

Daniel had died falling from the casino roof. Was it an accident or something more sinister? After the event, a note had been found, but it was written on a scrap of paper in unknown handwriting so could easily have been planted. But why would Daniel visit the roof when he was supposed to be collecting items from the catering van?

He would have known Vincent would be angry if he took too long, and visiting the roof on a whim was unlikely. No, Rose was sure he had gone to meet someone, and that he either slipped, perhaps trying to escape, or was pushed. His death solved a problem for his financial backer.

If Daniel had been paid to kill Aisha, then his employer was probably someone in Nairobi, who had a lot to lose from Aisha's continuing investigations and work at the Ethics and Anti-Corruption Commission. If this was the case, Rose knew it was out of her league and she would willingly hand the investigation back to Commissioner Akida.

As more evidence emerged during the investigation, Pearl had become the prime suspect. There was a lot of evidence including the earring on the casino roof, the hair braid clip clutched in her Aisha's fist and access to her mother's Mpesa account.

Like Daniel, she could easily have picked the muddler up from the bar and her whereabouts around the house were never fully explained on Saturday afternoon.

What motive did Pearl have? Money and independence came immediately to mind. There had been the argument on Saturday morning and Pearl must have been upset when her mother ordered Francis to leave.

And her anger could have increased when Aisha told her Francis was not actually interested in her, but in her mother's wealth and connections.

What Rose could not decide was whether Pearl had sufficient strength of character to kill her mother. She might have if she needed to defend herself, but Aisha would not have physically threatened her. Anyway, Rose was sure there was an element of planning to this murder.

She was getting nowhere, and her head started to spin. She closed her eyes and said a prayer for the Kafara family. The congregation stood as Father Matthew led the procession down the aisle and Rose concentrated on the readings, prayers and hymns of the service.

At the offertory hymn, she reached for her purse, but found she had absent-mindedly brought Aisha's black clutch bag. She opened it to find it still contained the collection of Crown Casino chips that Francis had inadvertently given her.

What would Father Matthew think if she put those in the collection bag?

She was about to close the bag when a flicker of candlelight illuminated something golden within.

She sifted through the chips until she found and removed a small gold disc, inlaid with a red stone. It was the matching half of the cufflink Thabiti had found on the roof of the casino. Now what was it doing in this bag?

The velvet collection bag passed to her, and she blushed as she put her hand inside, pretending to give a donation. Next week, she would need to double her offering. The remainder of the service passed Rose by as her mind attempted to make new connections.

At the end of the service, she stood and walked up the aisle with the rest of the congregation and looked towards the bright light at the entrance. Sunlight gleamed on the long blonde hair of the lady in the doorway. She hadn't expected to see Chloe at her church, but she hurried forward and tapped her on the shoulder.

"Chloe… Oh, sorry. I thought you were someone else." The lady gave a start and frowned before walking away with her friend. Rose remained in the church entrance, illuminated by sunlight, thinking about mistaken identities. With a flash of inspiration, she finally understood how, by whom, and probably why Aisha had been killed.

CHAPTER FIFTY-EIGHT

After church on Sunday morning, Rose turned abruptly into the yard of Guinea Fowl Cottage, sending a shower of dust into the air as she braked sharply, parking at a slant by the back gate.

She'd tried calling Thabiti from the church car park and he'd answered sleepily on the third attempt. She told him to get dressed, as she was driving straight over, but when she arrived, he was still in his pyjamas, sipping coffee lethargically at the dining table.

"Why are you not dressed? I told you we needed to hurry," she cried.

He squeezed his eyebrows together. "Why? What's the rush? It's Sunday morning."

She sat down, poured fresh coffee from a cafeteria into Thabiti's cup, and swallowed a mouthful.

"Er, what's going on?" He stammered as he leaned back.

"Is Pearl still in bed?" Rose countered.

"No, she left about ten minutes ago with Francis. I presume he's trying to patch things up."

Rose took another gulp of coffee and pushed the cup back to Thabiti. "I believe he's trying to cover things up, not patch them up."

Thabiti squeezed his eyes shut and rubbed them. "Cover up what? Please slow down and tell me what's going on."

Rose shook her head. "There's no time. Get dressed as quickly as you can. We need to find Pearl. I think she's in trouble."

Rose's anxiety must have displayed on her face as Thabiti suddenly stood up and said, "Give me two minutes."

Those two minutes helped Rose plan her next course of action. When Thabiti returned, dressed but still dishevelled, she asked, "Where's your Mother's gun? The one she shot me with."

"I locked it in the safe with the ammunition," he replied in an uneasy tone.

"Then fetch it."

"Is that really necessary?" Thabiti bit his lip.

"Trust me. I don't intend to use it, but we may need it for protection." Rose gulped at her words. Last time she had used a gun for protection, someone had died, but she steadied herself, remembering that she had not harmed anyone.

Thabiti retrieved the gun and reluctantly handed it over.

Rose returned to her Land Rover, climbed inside and loaded the pistol, but made sure the safety mechanism was on. "I don't want it to discharge by mistake."

She returned it to the bottom of an old canvas cartridge bag which contained essential first aid items. She might need some of them if matters got out of hand.

"Can you tell me where we're going?" Thabiti asked as Rose pulled onto the road.

"Timau."

Rose and Thabiti left Nanyuki and drove under the 'Welcome to Meru' sign, beyond the Nanyuki Show Ground. Rose braked just in time for the first speed bump, by a group of makeshift vegetable and timber stalls.

They drove for twenty minutes in silence until they reached Mia Moja, a small village south of Timau, which was alive with a Sunday clothes and vegetable market.

On the side of the road, a stallholder had woven trousers in and out of a wooden frame, creating an enticing display to attract passing traffic.

Rose slowed to avoid people chatting in groups on the roadside and swerved around an old woman making her arduous journey across the road.

Beyond the village, two policemen lounged under the shade of a couple of large fever trees. Across the road they'd placed two lengths of metal, with large protruding spikes, which was a typical Kenyan stopping point. But they ignored Rose as she carefully manoeuvred her Defender through the narrow gap between the pair of spikes and sped on.

Thabiti broke the silence. "But why Timau? Why would Francis bring Pearl here?"

"Because this is where it all started," declared Rose.

Thabiti looked out of the passenger window and muttered, "I still don't understand."

"I think you will soon. Now let me concentrate." Rose turned up the rutted dirt road leading to the Church of the Good Shepherd and onto a narrower track, parking behind a black Subaru Impreza outside Isaac's Hardware.

"Here we are."

"That's Francis's Subaru!" Thabiti glanced at the shop. "Is this his shop?"

"No, it's his father's, but it's where he grew up."

Rose took a deep breath and climbed down from her vehicle. She took her cartridge bag with her and secured it over her neck and across her shoulder. "Come on, but be quiet. We don't know what's going on inside."

CHAPTER FIFTY-NINE

Rose and Thabiti opened the door of Isaac's Hardware in Timau and found themselves beside a dusty counter. All was quiet and still.

Realising Thabiti was about to speak, Rose placed a finger to her lips. She lifted the wooden counter section and stepped through.

As she crept forward, she thought she heard moaning, but it wasn't coming from the shop. She heard the noise again, and it was soft, like a frightened animal which had been hunted, captured and restrained.

The noise became louder as she inched towards the rear of the shop and must be emanating from the store-cum-workshop beyond. She motioned to Thabiti, and they both stepped forward.

A sliver of light sliced the wall ahead of them, indicating that the connecting door was ajar. Rose peered into the next room and saw the back of a wooden chair and a figure slumped forward.

As she continued to watch, the person lifted their head. Rose closed and reopened her eyes. She was not too late. The figure, who she presumed was Pearl, was still alive.

Thabiti tried to push Rose aside, but she stood her ground, stared at him and shook her head. They both heard a voice from the next room. Francis's voice.

"I really am sorry about this, my sweet, but your usefulness has expired. I need to bury this unfortunate business and move on to a new life. There is much work to do within the Meru County Health Department, and I shall play a major part. Oh, you stare at me with such wide eyes."

Rose's eyes had adjusted to the gloom, and she watched Francis step in front of the chair, reach out with a hand, and stroke Pearl's cheek. Pearl flinched.

Thabiti shuffled from foot to foot, agitated and impatient, but Rose could not turn away from the sight next door, not yet.

"Did you think there would be a role for you? You are a pretty little thing, but you have no connections, no influence. Now your Ma is dead, you're just another attractive rich girl with too much time on your hands. What character could you play?"

The figure on the chair squirmed. She must be tied up. "No, I shall find myself a leading lady who can support my principal role. There are plenty who would like to join this hero on his journey."

The figure on the chair twisted again. "I know you were a great help, impersonating your mother and all those little clues you left lying about. Oh, you didn't know about those, did you? I'm surprised the commissioner didn't ask you about a pearl earring found on the casino roof. He must be more incompetent than I thought."

Rose mouthed at Thabiti, "Get ready."

When she looked again, Francis had his back to her. He turned around with a piece of green and red kanga material, which he was twisting into a thick rope. Was Francis really going to kill Pearl with her mother's headscarf?

"I promise to be quick, and if you don't fight, it won't be too painful. Don't worry, they will never find your body. All I need to do is call my friend Jeremiah, and your corpse will be burnt to ashes, just like your Ma's next Wednesday."

Francis stepped towards the chair and Pearl began twisting from side to side. She must be gagged as well as Rose could hear indiscriminate sounds rather than complete words. "Now, now, don't fight."

Rose turned to face a tense Thabiti who must have heard Francis's speech as his whole body was about to spring through the door. "Steady," whispered Rose. "Don't panic him."

Slowly and carefully, Rose opened the door to reveal herself and Thabiti. She put her hand out to the side, to prevent Thabiti rushing forward, and stood steadfastly, holding Francis's gaze. Francis squinted and Rose realised he might not be able to see them clearly in the gloom of the shop.

She stepped forward and said in an even tone, "It's time to stop, Francis. There have been enough deaths and this young woman has so much ahead of her."

"Death takes the young and the old," spat Francis. "What does it matter if I take one more life, or two?"

Thabiti stepped forward and Francis laughed. "Or three. The whole family and their interfering old friend. You have my admiration, though. When one of Jeremiah's contacts called Commissioner Akida and told him to drop the case, I thought that would be the end of it. And Thabiti's and your attempts to get to the truth were so clumsy that I'm amazed you're here. Did you just stumble on my whereabouts, or did you actually solve your case? Part of me would like to hear the explanation, but time is running out and my father will be back from church soon."

Thabiti spoke. "It's two against one. You've no chance."

Francis extracted a pistol from his suit jacket pocket and smiled wryly. "I think I have the advantage."

Rose froze. Now was the time to produce the gun she'd brought, but she couldn't move. Two guns and four people. The outcome could be devastating.

"Mama Rose," hissed Thabiti. She looked at his pleading eyes and down at his sister's head. At the sight of the gun, Pearl had started to rock the chair, and Rose was concerned she might capsize it. She stepped forward, placing a steadying hand on the chair and said, "It's OK. I'll take care of this."

Decision made, she reached into her cartridge bag and brought out the gun, clicked the safety mechanism and pointed it directly at Francis.

He laughed. "Aisha's gun! How resourceful of you, but what do you know about guns? I bet you've never fired one, never mind shot or killed anyone."

Rose studied Francis as she asked, "Have you, Francis? Shot someone, that is?" He hesitated a fraction.

"No, but I can add it to my list." His voice faltered, then he shrugged his shoulders and gazed back at Rose. "I'm prepared to do whatever is necessary. Are you?"

"Yes."

Thabiti added quickly, "She shot and killed a poacher forty years ago. I'm sure she's prepared to do it again." He glanced nervously at Rose.

"Actually, I didn't kill him, but for the past forty years I believed I had. I've lived with that guilt for so long, that replacing it with remorse for shooting you will be bearable. And I'm a good shot. I once had to shoot rabbits to feed my family."

Francis was looking around the group, frowning and unsure of himself.

Rose continued. "Sure, we could have a western-style stand-off and shoot each other. I might be injured, or worse. But I've lived a long life and to die protecting the children of one of my best friends, someone whose life I once saved, and who in turn saved me from prison, it's sort of fitting."

Rose raised her gun to point at Francis's head. He swallowed and mirrored the action, pointing his gun at Rose.

There was a deathly silence. Nobody dared move.

CHAPTER SIXTY

Rose waited, watching Francis. A minute passed in silence, then stretched to two minutes. The tension in the room fragmented as an old, stooped man shuffled into a pool of light shed by a standard lamp on the workbench.

"Son, what's going on? Why are you pointing a gun at Rose Hardie, and why is this young woman tied to my chair?" Nobody answered him. "Mama, you're not a police officer. Put that gun down."

"Sorry, I can't, Mr Isaac," replied Rose. "Your son has killed two people and I won't be responsible for any more deaths."

"Son, I don't know what this is about, but it needs to stop here. Life is too precious, too short, and it is not for us to destroy." Mr Isaac stepped between Rose and Francis, stretching an arm out towards each of them. Rose saw Francis crumple as he handed over his gun. She breathed in deeply, ejected the cartridge, and returned Aisha's gun to her bag.

Thabiti rushed to his sister and tugged at the tape covering her mouth. She yelped as he ripped it off. "I need something to cut the ropes," cried Thabiti.

"Look on the workbench," replied Mr Isaac, still watching his son.

Thabiti moved across to the workbench and Rose heard him scrabble about. He returned with a rusty knife whose blade was worn into a crescent shape.

He sawed away at the blue nylon rope restraining Pearl's hands until it finally frayed loose and Pearl shook her arms. She cradled them in her lap, whilst Thabiti worked at the binding on her feet.

When he finished, Mr Isaac said, "Young man, fetch some chairs. There is a stack of old wooden ones over by that wall. I need to sit down and I suspect Mama Rose does, too."

Rose was grateful for a seat, since she was beginning to feel cold and light-headed. She reached into her bag for her bottle of water and took a long swig. Pearl gestured for the bottle and gulped down most of its contents. They sat in a rough circle between Mr Isaac's stores.

Francis looked like a schoolboy with his head bowed, and his hands resting on his knees with his ankles crossed. He sat next to his father while Pearl and Thabiti were seated next to each other, separated from Rose by a stack of stone-coloured cement bags.

Mr Isaac, with his fluffy white hair, looked around the group with compassionate eyes. "Mama Rose, can you tell me what's been going on?"

Rose took a deep breath. "Let's start at the beginning. Here in this house and this shop." Mr Isaac looked surprised, and his body stiffened.

"A happy family struck by illness and tragedy. Bwana, you lost your wife and young daughter, but Francis lost his world, his beloved younger sister. Something changed within him, although he worked hard at school and achieved a scholarship to university."

Mr Isaac nodded. "Yes, I was very proud of him. He left to study economics at Meru University and from there obtained a coveted job in local government."

"Yes, but something happened." Rose addressed Francis's bowed head. "I suspect at some point it dawned on you that hard work was not enough. Perhaps someone less able was promoted because of their contacts. It happens all the time."

Francis looked up with a cold smile. "Thomas Wang'ethe." He looked back down at his hands.

Rose glanced around the group. "Francis sought wealth and influence and recognised he wouldn't achieve them through hard work alone. He made a point of meeting influential people, such as politicians and businessmen. And slowly his reputation spread as he met more important people and doors began to open for him. He was a bright and charismatic young man who was going places.

"In time he was introduced to Mr Jeremiah Angote, of the Modern Healthcare Group. Mr

Angote was expanding his business empire as the county governments were formed, and he needed ambitious local government employees to help him. Ones who were not averse to bending or even breaking the rules. In return, he introduced them to his contacts, and as equipment and service contracts were awarded, there were rewards in the form of bribes and backhanders."

Rose paused, looking round the group, but they were silent, waiting for her to continue. "But Francis made a mistake when he fell for a pretty girl at a party in Nairobi."

Rose looked towards Pearl. "Your mother was wrong. Francis was not attracted to you because of her money and influence. But then he discovered two things. Firstly, that your mother was a principal investigator with the Ethics and Anti-Corruption Committee, a body Francis wished to steer well clear of. And secondly, I'm afraid he perceived your wonderful childlike innocence and desire to please, which he could exploit to manipulate you.

"To start with, I think he just sought minor pieces of information, such as where your mother was planning to travel. But then I think he asked you to read documents your mother left out. I'm sure he gave you good reasons for wanting the details, such as staying ahead of the game, or giving him an advantage at work."

Pearl leaned against Thabiti, who wrapped a protective arm around her.

"Whatever information you told Francis, he fed back to Mr Angote," said Rose. "And at some point, it's likely your mother became suspicious, suspecting someone was reading her papers. Hoping to put a stop to it, she moved her family to Nanyuki." Rose paused and Thabiti pulled Pearl closer.

"I thought it strange your mother chose to stay in the guest cottage in the garden, rather than the main house. But I understand she became increasingly secretive and wouldn't even let Doris clean unless she was there. She may have guessed you were the one spying on her, Pearl, but it all came to a head on that fateful Saturday morning when she read the article about Mr Angote in the *Standard* newspaper."

Pearl turned to Rose. Her features were smooth and expressionless, but her eyes revealed a new depth, as if she was beginning to understand the duplicitous nature of life.

Rose turned back to Francis. "There you were, sitting at Aisha's table, smartly dressed and with money to spend. Money which she realised you weren't earning solely from your job in the county government and I think she guessed the truth and decided to investigate you. You know, she always hated people in power taking advantage of their positions, and her first step was to ban you from seeing Pearl."

Francis grunted, but Pearl spoke for the first time. "I was furious, but I had no idea about the article. Suddenly Ma was laying into Francis, calling him greedy, self-centred and untrustworthy. She told him to leave and never see me again. Here was an attractive, successful man who liked me, looked after me and gave me gifts, and she thought she could order him to go. It was not for her to make that decision."

Pearl started to cry as she shrugged off Thabiti's protective arm.

Rose speculated, "So you and Francis discussed matters and he persuaded you he'd done nothing wrong, and that your mother was confused and misinformed. Did he tell you he would speak to her and persuade her to change her mind?"

Pearl nodded and sobbed. "He did. He went to find Ma, but returned red in the face and shaking. He told me it had gone wrong, and that Ma had refused to listen. He said he'd become angry when she turned her back on him, but that he hadn't meant to hit her. He actually apologised when he told me he'd killed her." Pearl leaned against Thabiti for comfort, but he was rigid.

"As I thought," accepted Rose. "And he hid her body under a table in the catering tent."

"Hang on," said Thabiti, gesturing with his hand. "The body wasn't hidden. It was clearly visible on the floor of the tent. I saw it."

Rose shook her head. "Little is clear in this case. All the important elements are hidden."

CHAPTER SIXTY-ONE

The doors at either end of Mr Isaac's store swung open with such force that they bounced off the walls behind them. "Stop what you're doing. Hands up," shouted a police officer.

Gingerly, Rose raised her hands, and Thabiti and Pearl followed her lead. Mr Isaac nudged his son and helped him lift his hands above his head. Commissioner Akida strode into the room, wrinkling his brow.

He halted when he saw the small group and gave a shaky laugh. "No more dead bodies, Mama Rose. That's a relief. But looks like you're sitting around in the dark, conducting a seance."

"Commissioner, this is unexpected. And I see you've brought the heavy mob with you," replied Rose, raising her eyebrows.

"Constable Wachira was given a tip-off that you and Thabiti were seen rushing out of Nanyuki, and her contact was concerned about your safety."

Rose gave a slight laugh and thought to herself, that would be Sam. She wondered if he had drawn the same conclusion as her about the case. Somehow, she wouldn't be surprised if he had.

She looked up at the commissioner and suggested, "Why don't you pull up a chair?"

It was Thabiti who collected another chair and shuffled his own back to make room for the commissioner. Pearl curled up, wrapping her arms around her drawn-up knees.

Thabiti said, "Commissioner, Mama Rose was in the middle of explaining how and why Francis killed Ma and Daniel."

The commissioner leaned forward, staring at Rose. "Then please continue."

Rose scraped a hand through her hair. Her audience had grown. The arrival of the police meant the situation was secure, but somehow it made everything more formal.

She looked at Francis, but he was still slumped in his chair, looking at his hands, which he alternately clenched and unclenched.

"Commissioner, to recap. Aisha read an article in the *Standard* on the morning of her death. And she correctly linked the subject, Modern Healthcare Group and Jeremiah Angote, with Meru County Health Department. She suspected corruption, and that Francis was involved, but she needed evidence which would take time. Her immediate action was to ban Francis from seeing Pearl."

The commissioner nodded his understanding.

Rose continued, "This must have been a disaster for Francis. Not only had he lost the ability to source information, which was proving valuable to Mr Angote, but if Aisha investigated the Meru County Health Department, he could lose everything and even go to jail. He followed Aisha into the catering tent and when she refused to listen, he hit her on the back of the head with the muddler he had picked up from the makeshift bar."

The commissioner closed his gaping mouth and, with a wry smile, shook his head.

Rose took a breath. "Crucially, this was not at six o'clock, as Francis made us believe. But I would guess about an hour earlier, when Thabiti was out of the house and the catering staff were busy with their preparations."

The commissioner removed his penknife and began whittling away on another small piece of wood. He asked, "How do you know this?"

"I just couldn't make the facts fit. Francis tried to implicate Daniel, and then Pearl. Both had the opportunity to commit the crime, but somehow it didn't fit right in my mind, or my mind was taking into account the whole jigsaw, even though some pieces were missing. Doris commented that Aisha must have put up a fight as her fist was clenched, and when Thabiti and I viewed her body at the mortuary, we saw that Doris was right."

The commissioner nodded absentmindedly.

Rose said, "Rigor mortis is not immediate and shortly after death, the muscles in the body actually become soft and flaccid. Rigor mortis is when the muscles become firm and rigid, and begin with the smaller muscles, including those of the hands. And higher temperatures speed up the process. The time between Aisha's last supposed appearance at around six, and the discovery of her body was only about five minutes, a maximum of ten. That's not enough time for the rigor mortis process to begin, even in our hot climate. The level of stiffness was more in line with a body that had been dead for at least half an hour."

Rose paused to let the information sink in.

Mr Isaac viewed his son with dull eyes.

Thabiti stood and examined the tools on the workbench.

Rose continued, "At the mortuary, we discovered why Aisha's fist was clenched. She was clasping a silver guinea fowl feather hair braid clip, one that belonged to Pearl. This was probably Francis's biggest mistake. He had placed the clip in Aisha's palm and closed her hand around it, trying to implicate Pearl. But he actually highlighted that the body had been dead for some time."

Thabiti stabbed a chisel into a block of wood.

Rose noticed Pearl was very pale, with a pink tint to her cheeks. Poor girl, even when she was trying to help Francis, he was scheming against her. Rose strengthened her resolve and continued in a firmer and clearer voice.

"After Francis hit Aisha, he checked that she was dead, rolled her body under the table, and covered it. He removed her headscarf, which he needed for his deception plan. I think he admitted to Pearl that he'd killed her mother, but explained it away as an accident. Perhaps he played on the advantages, such as Pearl being free of her mother's control, but meanwhile, he continued his duplicitous plan. He planted the murder weapon in the top of Pearl's chest of drawers and removed one of her pearl earrings, in case he needed to plant further evidence."

Pearl looked at Rose and stammered, "But both my earrings are missing, and the box containing them."

Rose leaned over and placed a conciliatory hand on her leg. "Yes, I know. I will come to that. Francis can certainly think on his feet, and his plan was ingenious. Aisha had been given a large piece of kanga material from which she had skirts made for herself and Pearl. Pearl's had not been ready, but I think Francis called the tailor, instructing him to finish the skirt and deliver it to the cottage. Doris told me it arrived on Saturday, and it was the skirt she ironed, and was carrying to Pearl, when Vincent, the chef, bumped into her and spilt the tea."

Thabiti picked up a hook-shaped tool and examined it.

"Francis instructed Pearl to visit her mother's guest cottage, on the pretence of borrowing a necklace. She wore a dressing gown to cover the kanga skirt she was wearing. In the guest cottage, she borrowed one of Aisha's shirts and arranged a couple of pillows under it to give the impression of Aisha's larger frame. Pearl's disguise would not have stood up to scrutiny, but it was timed so she was only viewed from afar. And I was the witness for this charade."

Thabiti knocked over a light, which crashed onto the table. "Sorry!" He stood the lamp on its base, illuminating the seated group.

Rose continued, "Pearl left the guest cottage, and Francis called to her using Aisha's name, so I assumed the figure was Aisha. My eyesight is far from perfect, and I saw a well-proportioned African woman wearing a red and green kanga skirt and one of Aisha's hallmark matching turban headscarves. I assumed it was Aisha, since Francis called out her name, and although I didn't hear a response, I saw the figure raise a hand and walk round to the back of the house."

CHAPTER SIXTY-TWO

Mr Isaac walked to the back of his store and collected a bag of brightly coloured sweets which he passed around. The commissioner unwrapped one whilst staring at Rose.

Thabiti returned to his seat and helped himself to a handful of sweets, which he placed in his lap.

Rose declined the offered bag as she wanted to complete her explanation as quickly and clearly as she could, and return to the sunlight outside.

She continued, "In the tent, Pearl removed the headscarf and cushions, hiding them from view. Doris found the pillows later, but presumed someone had been sleeping in the tent. Pearl uncovered her mother's body and rolled it out from its hiding place under the table, so it could be discovered by whoever entered the tent next."

"She returned to her bedroom through the kitchen when Doris saw her, but didn't understand the significance. Pearl quickly changed into a dress and appeared on the veranda where Francis and I were talking. She asked Francis to help fasten the zip on her dress."

Rose could see Thabiti walk through the steps in his mind as he beat and wagged a finger.

The commissioner examined the dusty ceiling.

"Daniel discovered the body," said Rose. "He was a frequent visitor to the tent. Once the shock of seeing Aisha dead had worn off, he recognised the significance of what he'd seen earlier: Francis following Aisha into the tent. He correctly guessed Francis killed her. As Daniel had no love for the Onyango family, or the authorities, he confronted Francis to blackmail him. I think it was Daniel, returning to speak to Francis, that I saw out of the corner of my eye as I left Guinea Fowl Cottage on Saturday evening. To ensure

Daniel's immediate silence, Pearl sent Mpesa from her mother's phone."

The commissioner nodded, "As we suspected."

"Francis later admitted to being short of money, so I suspect Daniel demanded more money for his continued silence. Perhaps Francis realised Daniel would continue to drain him of funds, or Daniel asked for another payment. Either way, Francis went to the casino early to give Daniel a note to meet him on the roof. I've no idea what happened up there and I doubt Francis is ready to enlighten us."

Francis remained silent.

His father slowly shook his head.

"Daniel fell from the roof and died, which solved Francis's witness problem. He took Pearl's earring and hid it on the roof, under the caterer's van keys, which he had seen Daniel drop."

The commissioner frowned. "I was not aware that an earring had been found."

"That's my fault, sorry," mumbled Thabiti through the sweet he sucked. He did not meet the commissioner's gaze. "I spotted it, and thinking it might be one of Pearl's, gave it to Mama Rose to check for me, which she did."

Rose screwed up her mouth. "I wasn't convinced Pearl had dropped it. When we saw her that evening, she was upset and had a red mark on her arm. But I didn't know if it was from an altercation with Daniel on the roof, or with Francis for his pursuit of another woman. I think it was the latter."

Pearl nodded and rocked in her chair. "He barely spoke to me that night, although he seemed elated, laughing and joking with other people. He was almost manic, and gambling, which I'd never seen him do before. He was always so controlled, but not that night. And once he was introduced to the President's niece, I didn't get a look in."

Rose looked across at Pearl. "He saw me arrive and joined us, probably to check what we were discussing. When he heard your mother's will had been found, but your inheritance would be managed through a trust, he probably realised you were no longer of use to him."

Pearl hid her face in her knees and her shoulders shook. Thabiti patted her back and unwrapped another sweet.

Rose said, "Francis made another mistake, which he was unaware of. During whatever altercation occurred on the roof, he broke a cufflink. Thabiti found part of it on the roof, near the earring. He didn't report it to you, Commissioner, as he didn't think it was important."

The commissioner puffed up his chest and said, "In the future, I will be the one to judge if a piece of evidence is important or not."

Rose made a conciliatory gesture with her hands. "I only understood the relevance of it this morning, when I found the other half. Whilst I was talking to Pearl at the casino, Francis mistakenly filled my bag, rather than Pearl's, with gambling chips. I found the bag this morning, and in it the missing half of the cufflink which Francis had dropped. It was the final clue. But I was worried Francis no longer needed Pearl, and since she knew too much, he might seek to silence and kill her. I rushed round to Guinea Fowl Cottage and found she had already left with Francis."

Thabiti raised his eyebrows. "How did you know where he'd taken Pearl? I would never have looked here."

Rose repeated her earlier statement. "This is where it all began."

Rose looked across at Mr Isaac, who appeared even older, almost ghostlike. She hoped this incident would not send him to his grave. "How old was Francis when his mother and sister died, Mr Isaac?"

"Twelve. Francis was very protective of his younger sister, and when she died, he became quiet, withdrawing into his own world. As you said, he worked hard at school, but with a fevered anguish. Looking back, I guess he blamed himself, and he definitely blamed me. He was always angry: angry about our poverty, and angry that his mother and his darling sister Sarah could not be saved."

For the first time since the commissioner had arrived, Francis looked up. His cheeks were stained with tears, and his eyes were hollow and haunted.

He said, "You were always working in your shop, whatever the hour, doing someone else's bidding. Fetching, ordering, and delivering for your customers. But when Ma and Sarah fell ill, you didn't have the money for medicine, for dawa to save them. You couldn't even afford hospital treatment, so you brought them back here to die." Francis raged at his father, his cheeks were flushed and he had a sheen on his skin.

His father looked back with pity. He placed a hand on Francis's leg, but Francis yanked it away.

In a quiet, soothing voice, Mr Isaac replied, "I brought them home at your mother's request. She didn't want to die alone in a sombre, cold ward, away from Sarah, from us. She wanted to be at home, where she felt comfortable. Here she accepted her fate and found peace."

"But the dawa. You gave her no medicine," Francis raged.

Mr Isaac shook his head sadly. "There was nothing I could give either of them, apart from some painkillers. They contracted viral meningitis. And so did you, but yours was less severe, and you recovered after a week. They were both admitted to hospital, but antibiotics do not work against viruses. There was nothing the doctors could do except make them comfortable."

Tears ran down his face. "Most people recover, like you, but they did not. In the end, they both stopped eating and had very little energy."

Francis looked utterly drained and seemed to have reverted to the twelve-year-old boy he once was. He stretched out his hand, took hold of his father's, and squeezed.

CHAPTER SIXTY-THREE

R ose blinked in the bright sunshine as she stepped out of Mr Isaac's hardware shop in Timau. She shivered despite the heat of early afternoon.

A policeman accompanied Thabiti, who followed Rose, with his arm wrapped protectively around his sister. Another policeman supported Francis out of the shop, and the commissioner emerged conversing quietly with Mr Isaac.

The commissioner turned to Thabiti and called, "Your sister will need to come with us. There are many details to fill in and questions requiring answers. I am afraid she will be spending the next few days in prison."

Rose interrupted him. "Commissioner, can I suggest that instead of prison, you keep her on a secure ward at the Cottage Hospital? I doubt she has been looking after herself and with the stress of her mother's death and our investigation I don't think she's been eating properly."

The commissioner looked across at Pearl, who resembled a limp lily. "I'll see how she stands up to questioning. It might be a sensible idea if she begins to wilt. From your explanation, it appears she acted as an accessory after the fact, but that still carries a custodial sentence. We need to establish if she was coerced or pressured in any way."

The commissioner gestured to Rose, and they both stepped away from the group. "I suspect I may be able to justify dropping the charges against Pearl. A storm will erupt once it's known someone from the Deputy Inspector General's Office contacted me to call off the formal murder investigation. Interfering in the workings of the law is serious, very serious indeed."

Rose replied, "I'm just relieved we've finally discovered the truth and that poor, misguided Francis won't be causing any more deaths."

"Surely you don't feel sorry for him?" The commissioner removed his cap.

"Of course I do. His adolescent mind drew the wrong conclusion from the situation it witnessed. And that shaped Francis's entire life, leading to this terrible tragedy. Had he known the truth, and that his sister and mother could not be saved, then none of this would have happened."

The commissioner ran his hands through his hair and replaced his cap. "I need to process the suspects and create a formal record of the case. What about you?"

"I'm hungry," said Rose.

Thabiti wandered over. "Did someone mention food? I'm starving, but aren't we too late for lunch?"

"I'll call Craig, and he can ask Kipto to make something for us."

Rose walked back to the shop entrance and stood opposite Mr Isaac. She clasped both his hands in hers and said, "Bwana, you have my deepest sympathy.

Life has dealt you a harsh hand. Please don't wonder what might have been, or if you could have done things differently."

Slowly, she climbed into her Defender, feeling deflated.

Thabiti climbed in beside her. "OK?" he asked.

"Yes." She nodded and started the engine.

CHAPTER SIXTY-FOUR

R ose lay along the outdoor sofa on her patio and looked up at the old wooden roof beams. She felt conflicted.

Whilst Aisha and Daniel's deaths were tragic, she accepted she could not have prevented them. The players were already at the table and the pack shuffled before she arrived at Aisha's party. Indeed, the cards had been dealt as Aisha was already dead. She shuddered.

As for Daniel, had he told the police, or her, that he had seen Francis follow Aisha into the tent, he would still be alive but instead, he chose to play the game, to gamble, and he had lost.

She was relieved Pearl had not been seriously injured. She had acted as the dummy hand, her part in the game controlled by Francis, and Rose hoped the commissioner would show compassion when interviewing her.

As for herself, she was back to plain old Mama Rose, the community vet. Again, part of her was relieved, but it had been exciting piecing together clues and starting to understand, a little better, how people thought and why they acted the way they did.

In the future, she must remember not to judge a book by its cover. That a man begging on the street, or a child stealing food, would have a story to tell, and a reason for their actions, even if it was morally flawed.

What about Mr Kafara's grandson? Were his reasons for demanding money from her justified? He knew his father had been acting illegally, as he was a poacher, but probably not that the gang planned to kidnap and kill. His asking for money for a past crime was not unusual.

The British Government had agreed to pay over twenty million pounds to Kenyans tortured by

British Colonial Forces during the Mau Mau uprising some sixty years ago.

Rose preferred to repay the debts she owed with her own time. It was probably what drove her to help members of the local community, whether it was through rabies vaccination clinics, her visits to the women of Nanyuki prison with clothes, underwear and food, or helping at the refuge for teenage mums.

She had known suffering and with determination and the help of others, she had overcome it. It was her duty to help those less fortunate than herself.

Thabiti had collected the two boxes of Aisha's clothes from the alley by the casino, which she now needed to distribute. She would visit the teenage mums this week and Nanyuki Prison next week.

Thabiti had devoured his lunch, thanked Rose, and left for the police station. He had accepted her suggestion to go via Guinea Fowl Cottage and pack a bag for Pearl.

Thabiti had been elated over lunch, grinning and laughing, but Rose suspected his euphoria would soon wear off.

The relief of finding Pearl alive, and the satisfaction of helping to bring his mother's killer to justice, would give way to grief and depression.

Rose would need to keep an eye on him this week and ensure he didn't seek solace in a bottle again. She prayed Pearl would not be confined to prison where she could so easily waste away and become a shadow.

CHAPTER SIXTY-FIVE

"May I disturb you?" came the soft drawl of a voice. Rose sat up to find Sam standing at the edge of the patio.

"Sam, welcome. Take a seat, whilst I tell Craig you're here. He'll want to hear all your news."

"Dear lady, stay where you are," replied Sam. "You've had an eventful day and no doubt need some rest. I'll speak to Craig. Where can I find him?"

Rose pointed. "Just through that door, in the living room. I suspect he's watching horse racing on TV."

Rose tidied the remains of lunch on the outdoor dining table and arranged tea and coffee things with the flask of boiling water Kipto had left.

When Sam reappeared, he was helping Craig with one hand and carrying two tins of Tusker in the other. He made sure Craig was sitting comfortably before pouring their beers into glasses.

Rose made a soothing cup of tea and said, "I guess you sent the cavalry this morning, Sam?"

The large man grinned. "I spotted you driving past Nanyuki Showground. You had such a determined look on your face that I was certain you'd reached a crucial point in your investigation."

Rose studied him shrewdly through partially closed eyes. "Had you solved the case?"

Sam leaned back and pushed his feet out in front of him. "Whilst catching up with colleagues in Nairobi on Saturday, I heard there had been a commotion at the Deputy Inspector General's Office. An employee was discovered sending false emails and making bogus calls. The rumours allege he was linked to Jeremiah Angote's Modern Healthcare Group, so it made me wonder about the legitimacy of that call to the commissioner instructing him to close Aisha's case."

Rose's eyes widened. "So they know about the call, or at least they soon will. The inspector said the fake call was likely to be of more concern to the authorities than Aisha's murder, though, of course, they are linked. Did you know it was Francis?"

"Who else could it be? But I couldn't understand how he did it. I still can't."

Rose explained how Francis had used Pearl to create a deception and impersonate her mother.

"Ingenious, really," declared Sam. "I'm relieved that it's over, that the killer has been caught, and that you are no longer in danger. I can return to my day job without having to worry about you."

Rose started. "I didn't know you worried about me. Thank you." She sipped her tea. "What aspect of the day job are you returning to do?"

"Next month is the inaugural Giants Club Summit here in Nanyuki. There's a lot of preparation work, and some of it is undercover."

Craig asked, "What of your meeting in Nairobi with the man from Mombasa?"

"That's the real reason I'm here," replied Sam, leaning back in his chair. "We had our meeting, and whilst he was reticent at the beginning, he slowly opened up. I think he realised I only wanted to know about that particular incident. I had the impression he hadn't agreed with the way it was handled, as he said something along the lines of 'kidnapping women is not my way of doing business'."

Sam paused and swallowed a mouthful of beer. "He confirmed that his group had been approached by a politician. Someone they wanted to ingratiate themselves with, as they correctly saw his political potential and future usefulness. His group was asked to send men to Ol Kilima to meet up with some poachers and he was one of the men sent. He confirmed they were not there to poach, but to kidnap the daughter of one of Josiah Kariuki's leading supporters. They thought it would be simple, as they waited until Craig left the farm before making their approach. The last thing they had expected was for you to start shooting."

Sam grinned at Rose, but it wasn't something she could joke about. "The local men panicked and ran away, and the Nairobi men were forced to retreat. The blood found at the site was from a graze caused when the teenager ran into the wall in alarm. The local guys were agitated, and one demanded more money, because he knew why the men were there and wanted payment for his silence."

Once again, Rose recognised how fortunate they had been, and reminded herself she had taken the correct action.

Sam crossed his ankles. "The Mombasa man said they were an emerging organisation and could not surrender to such demands made by country folk. They shot the local man as a warning, not only to the other poachers, but to other criminals, to show they were not to be messed with."

Rose asked, "What about the money paid to the widow?"

"Ironic, I think. Hush money paid after the man had been silenced."

Craig attempted to sit up.

"Thank you, Sam, for all you've done. We've carried the heavy burden of guilt for the past forty years and it's a relief to know what really happened."

"When will we see you next?" Rose asked as she leant forward.

"Who knows, but I will be looking out for you." Sam stood. "Thank you for the beer."

He smiled and walked away, whistling.

CHAPTER SIXTY-SIX

On Monday morning, as Rose sipped her first cup of tea, she received a call summoning her to Dua Kali, a village twenty minutes west of Nanyuki. Her patient, a cow, had been attacked by a lion.

The call came from a European lady who Rose had not met and who was probably new to the area and didn't know how to protect her animals from predators. Rose mentally shook her head. She must not prejudge the situation or the people involved.

The area she drove through was exceptionally dry with only sparse tufts of yellowing grass scattered between thorn bushes. Small herds of zebra and impala usually roamed the open bush-land, adjoining the road, but the lack of vegetation had driven them away in search of forage.

Predators in the area, such as large cats, would certainly be suffering from a lack of prey, and attacks on farm and domestic animals were not uncommon in such circumstances.

Rose turned off the road and beeped her horn at a flat green metal gate. Security appeared to be tight, so her initial thoughts might be wrong. An attractive couple who Rose judged to be in their fifties greeted her at the front of a single-storey stone house.

"Thank you so much for coming at short notice and before breakfast," said the lady. "I'm Bridget and this is my partner, Harvey."

The man extended his hand. "Harvey Brightman."

Rose followed the couple as Bridget said, "You saw our night watchman. We can't blame the fellow. He said he smelt lion and as soon as the guinea fowl squawked their warning, he made a run for it and hid in his guard hut."

Behind the house was a dark-soiled field with a smaller enclosure at one end. "We'd been warned of a lion escaping from Ol Pejeta Conservancy, and a horse was attacked several nights ago. We only have five cattle, but we started building a stronger corral. Unfortunately, we haven't finished it," said Harvey.

Rose surveyed the nearly complete structure of mismatched poles, cut from the surrounding bush, and dug into the ground so they stood upright, side by side, to a height of some six feet. There was a two metre gap where the original fence and gate stood.

"He must have got in over here," Bridget said, opening the gate. "We were planning to finish the corral today."

Inside, Rose found a cow standing on some hay scattered over the crumbly earth, with large rips along her side and flank. Her head lolled. It was obvious by the parallel scratch lines that the rips were caused by the lion's claws.

Lions grab their victims high up, sinking their claws in to gain leverage, and then they throw them bodily to the ground.

"My primary concern is infection," said Rose. "Lions' claws are fetid places, which carry the remains of previous kills. Please, can I have a bucket half-filled with warm water, and two plastic bowls?"

In the first bowl, Rose poured a small amount of liquid iodine. She added warm water until the diluted mixture was the colour of iced tea, and removed strips of old towel from her bag. After the procedure, the strips would be soaked in disinfectant before being boil-washed.

Rose submerged a piece of towel, wrung it out, and wiped it across a lion scratch. She repeated the process until she had cleaned all the wounds. Then she took a clean piece of towel and re-washed the wounds.

To her clients, she explained, "The iodine solution removes bacteria." Whilst the wound dried, Rose added some powdered Tryponil to more warm water.

"I'll wash the wounds again with this solution, which cleans away any diseases left by flies."

Rose finished by sprinkling powdered Tryponil over the wounds to prevent new flies or ticks infecting them.

She said, "Watch the wounds closely and call me if they become red, start weeping or swelling, or if the cow appears to have a fever." She injected the cow with Betamox, a penicillin-based antibiotic, to fight against bacterial infection.

As she started to pack her bag, her phone pinged, and she opened a message from Thabiti. Commissioner Akida had asked to meet them at Dormans in an hour.

CHAPTER SIXTY-SEVEN

Hammering. Thabiti felt it inside his head. He also heard it. The noise resumed. Someone was impatiently bashing the back door. Reluctantly, he climbed out of bed, stumbled through the house, and opened the door.

An efficient-looking gentleman in a green uniform, with a matching peaked cap, thrust an envelope and a clipboard at him. Thabiti dropped the letter, but scrawled his name on the clipboard.

The man nodded curtly and strode back to his green liveried van with a yellow star. Pixel scampered out of the door, collected the envelope in her teeth, and dashed back into the house.

"Pixel, heel. That's my letter." Pixel eyed him before trotting back and dropping her package at his feet. She sat down and thumped her tail on the floor.

Thabiti immediately recognised the crest of Central University, Nairobi. He held the envelope between a finger and thumb, contemplating whether to drop it straight in the bin. Pixel yapped. She was hungry.

Thabiti delayed his decision, carrying the envelope to the kitchen where he deposited it on a worktop.

The news of Pearl's abduction and subsequent arrest had completely exhausted Doris. Yesterday afternoon she'd informed him she was taking a week's leave. She'd reappeared wearing a light blue polyester suit, and carrying a brown suitcase with a multi-coloured belt wrapped around it.

Thabiti watched her leave on the back of a boda-boda and wondered if she would ever return.

Pixel yapped again.

He found her dog biscuits and supplemented them with some canned meat. The moment he placed her bowl on the floor, she stuck her head in and practically inhaled its contents. Thabiti felt the heat of the letter burning his back, so he turned to stare at it.

As if to delay discovery, he carefully cut through the top of the envelope and slowly extracted the letter. He smoothed it out and read.

'This letter hereby notifies Thabiti Onyango (the student) that all charges pertaining to the student's alleged misconduct towards another pupil, Peggy Mwathi, have been dropped.'

'The student's suspension from the university ceases with immediate effect, and we ask the student to contact us, at his earliest convenience, to discuss his continuing education at Central University...'

No apology, no explanation.

He turned the letter over and found a scribbled note. "Your hat was discovered in James Hatia's cupboard by his room-mate. James was confronted and confessed to assaulting Peggy because she refused his advances."

There was no name or signature. Thabiti turned the envelope upside down and shook it, but there was nothing else.

He sat alone on the veranda, staring into the garden.

So that's that. He could return to normal life, but what was that?

Ma was gone and Pearl could be imprisoned. He was not sure he wanted to return to university, not sure what he really wanted to do.

He smiled. He had time. Time to think, time to relax, time to decide what was important to him. Pixel appeared, licking her jaw. Time for breakfast—that was important to him right now.

CHAPTER SIXTY-EIGHT

There was ample space to park in front of Dormans coffee shop on Monday morning. Rose was surprised to see Thabiti already seated at a table, wearing a ludicrous red and yellow striped beanie hat and drinking a brightly coloured juice.

He said, "Banana and strawberry smoothie to jump start my body. I've also ordered a fried breakfast, as I'm starving. Doris is taking the week off to see her family and recover from the events of the past few weeks."

Rose asked, "Are you going to keep her on? Will you return to Nairobi?"

Thabiti grinned. "I have some great news. I received a letter from the university this morning confirming that the investigation has been completed. Apparently, another student spotted my hat in his room-mate's cupboard. They discovered the victim refused to go on a date with the boy, which embarrassed him, and he admitted to attacking her. But I've still no idea why he used my hat and implicated me."

Rose sighed. "Another case of deception, but congratulations. Are you returning to university then?"

Thabiti sucked pink liquid through a straw. "I don't know. I'm not sure exactly what I want to do."

The waitress appeared at their table. "A cup of Kericho Gold, please." Rose's tummy rumbled, reminding her she had left home before breakfast. "And eggs Benedict. I shall join you for breakfast, Thabiti."

Thabiti continued. "I think I'll stay up here, certainly until Ma's case has been concluded. And Pearl will need time to recover, which will be easier in Nanyuki, which has a better climate and is less hectic than Nairobi. I've realised just how little I know about the world so I think I'll get a job or something, and then I might return to uni, when I know what I really want to do."

Thabiti's breakfast arrived at the same time as Commissioner Akida, who commented, "That looks good. I'm so hungry I could eat a hairy buffalo." He ordered a fried English breakfast with two poached eggs and a large cappuccino.

The commissioner sat down and said, "Before I start with all the thank you's, let me update you. Francis confessed to everything. Gone is his confident manner and immaculate turnout and he's so distraught that I believe he is reliving his sister's death. I can't get him to eat anything so I may have to send him to hospital as well, if things don't improve."

"As well. Does that mean Pearl is already in hospital?" asked Rose.

"Yes, you were right," admitted the commissioner. "She was completely exhausted and fainted on the journey back to Nanyuki. We took her straight to hospital and put her on a drip."

"You don't look too concerned about your sister." Rose addressed Thabiti, who had just stuffed a large mouthful of egg and sausage into his mouth.

The commissioner laughed a deep belly laugh as Thabiti chewed self-consciously. "That's probably because we are not pursuing charges against Pearl. Francis admitted that he coerced Pearl into impersonating her mother and pressured her into keeping quiet and pay Daniel and I think she acted out of naivety and love rather than malice. Besides, there are other important fish to fry."

"Thanks," spluttered Thabiti. "I hope Pearl will reconsider her relationship with Ma, and understand that she was just trying to protect us, even if she was rather heavy-handed."

"Will she be in hospital for long?" asked Rose.

Thabiti nodded. "Physically, she needs some rest and to regain some weight. But most of the damage is mental, from Francis persuading her to take part in the murder of her own mother. Dr Farrukh thinks she will need to stay in hospital for several weeks, or even a month. She is very vulnerable at the moment and it will be hard for her to face the world again."

422

"Back to Francis. What will happen to him?" asked Rose.

"A quick closed trial as he is not contesting the charges and has admitted his guilt."

"What about Mr Jeremiah Angote? Does he face any charges?" Rose pressed.

"I am not sure what they can charge him with. Hopefully, other government officials will recognise that all that glitters is not gold when it comes to Mr Angote."

Rose and the commissioner's food and drinks arrived, and for a time, they ate in silence.

The commissioner said, "There is to be a purge of employees at the Deputy Inspector General's Office, though. They'll keep it quiet, but it's rattled a few cages." He chewed another mouthful.

Rose was enjoying her eggs Benedict. It was the first time in over a week that she was able to sit quietly and enjoy a meal.

The commissioner wiped his mouth. "Of course I am hugely grateful to you, Mama Rose, for your hard work and intuition in solving this case."

Thabiti sat up. "And you too, Thabiti. I'll have to call on you again when I have a puzzling case."

"Cooee," came the cry. Rose looked up to see a brightly coloured Chloe standing by their table. "How's the sleuthing going?"

Chloe noticed the commissioner. "Oh, I like a man in uniform." She gave the commissioner a warm, open smile and sat down opposite him.

"Case closed," said Rose.

"Well done. Tell me all about it."

The commissioner puffed out his chest. He engaged Chloe with a long and detailed account of the case, allowing Rose to finish her breakfast in peace, drifting with her own thoughts.

CHAPTER SIXTY-NINE

On Wednesday, Rose and Craig joined Thabiti, Pearl and Commissioner Akida at Cape Chestnut restaurant. They were a sombre group, having attended Aisha's cremation, and they sat at a wooden table under the shade of a cape chestnut tree, after which the small restaurant was named.

Rose was thoughtful. She had once attended a cremation in the UK, where the crematorium, although stark and impersonal, was clean and efficient.

The coffin rolled through to a rear area, the hatch doors closed and music played whilst the final business took place out of view.

Aisha's cremation was very different. A bonfire was constructed in a yard surrounded by crumbling concrete walls. The coffin was placed on top and the pyre set alight, like the photos her daughter Heather used to send from the UK of Guy Fawkes night.

"A toast," Commissioner Akida called. He stood at the end of the table, resplendent in his best navy uniform. "As Rosa Parks, the first lady of the American civil rights movement said, 'I would like to be known as a person who is concerned about freedom and equality and justice and prosperity for all people.' I'm sure that's how Aisha would wish us to remember her. So please raise your glasses to Aisha."

Thabiti helped Pearl stand, but Craig shook his head. Rose knew he was tired from standing round the bonfire waiting for the flames to consume Aisha's coffin.

Even now, Rose expected to see small particles of debris flit in the surrounding air.

She raised her glass with the others and called, "Aisha."

The commissioner approached Thabiti. "I'm glad we could release your mother's body in the knowledge justice has been served. But now I must return to my office."

To Rose and Craig, he said, "Thank you again for your help. And enjoy your lunch."

A white-shirted waiter approached their table and placed the restaurant's speciality, fillet steak, chips and mixed vegetables, in front of Rose and Craig. Another waiter brought steak for Thabiti and a chicken salad for Pearl.

Rose watched Pearl peck at her salad. She was pale and her eyes looked haunted and sunken into the hollows of their sockets. She had not spoken to anyone apart from Thabiti, who she only whispered to.

"Thabiti," said Craig. "Rose has to catch up with her vet work after all this sleuthing, so I wondered if you would join me for an hour or so each morning, for coffee and help me with a crossword."

He leaned towards Thabiti and lowered his voice. "And I need some male company. Rose and Kipto do fuss."

Rose silently applauded Craig. They were both concerned for Thabiti, who was living on his own, mourning his mother and worrying about his sister without the distraction of work or study. If he visited Craig each morning, they could keep an eye on him.

"Sounds good to me," said Thabiti. His voice was strained, but he gave Craig a weak smile. Both Thabiti and Pearl needed time to heal.

CHAPTER SEVENTY

After lunch, Rose and Craig returned home. Rose sat back on the large cedar sofa, looking out over the garden. The mountain was hidden behind a cloud and the afternoon had prematurely darkened.

Rose alternately stroked Izzy and Potto, who were intertwined next to her. Izzy purred deeply and satisfyingly.

The commissioner had been joking, she was sure, when he suggested she help in future cases, but would she want to, if he asked?

Investigations were time consuming, tiring and potentially dangerous, but this one had satisfied her, especially knowing that justice had been served. She felt an inner glow. Life would seem just a little duller without the excitement of the case.

She also felt lighter, and blessed Sam for revealing the truth about the events at Ol Kilima. It was time to seek redemption and confess her sins. She would visit Father Matthew in the morning.

"Mama." Kipto interrupted her thoughts. "Nice flowers come for you." Kipto placed a bunch of old English roses, which she had already arranged in a vase, on the table and handed a large envelope to Rose.

Inside was a note: "Thank you for saving Gertrude, from Bridget and Harvey Brightman" and a colourful children's book entitled *How the Guinea Fowl Got her Spots.*

Rose opened the book, enjoying the illustrations, and started to read. Guinea Fowl and Cow were two friends who shared a common enemy, Lion. After Guinea Fowl, a plain brown bird, saved Cow from Lion a second time, Cow splashed drops of cream onto Guinea Fowl, which dried into white spots.

Lion came across the speckled bird and asked if she knew Guinea Fowl. Rose laughed at the deception, as Lion did not look beyond the spots, at the bird below.

In praise of the story, the heavens opened and a deluge of rain fell, the noise on the tin mabati roof sounding like an audience applauding.

Do you love elephants? Mama Rose does, but an international wildlife conference she attends is threatened when the principal speaker is found dead in her hotel room.

With Commissioner Akida tied up in Nairobi, Rose starts tracking down clues, but can she trap the murderer before she ends up as the next target?

Buy Tusk Justice to hunt down a predator today!

Would you like to know more about Mama Rose and her hometown, Nanyuki?

Download her exclusive interview, and receive regular updates from me.

Or Download at https://bookfunnel.victo-riatait.com/qygp9guqmp

If you enjoyed this book, please tell someone you know. And for those people you don't know, leave a review to help them decide whether or not to read it.

Click the QR Code, or visit the store you bought this book from.

For more information visit VictoriaTait.com

CPSIA information can be obtained
at www.ICGtesting.com
Printed in the USA
BVHW031937210123
656727BV00003B/736